Oprah

Winfrey

Hates

My Guts

(A Holiday Romantic Comedy)

by

Terry MacMillian/T.R. Locke

Media City PUBLISHERS

Oprah Winfrey Hates My Guts
Copyright ©2017 Terry MacMillian/T.R.Locke and Media
City Publishers

ISBN-13: 978-1981260119
ISBN-10: 1981260110
BISAC: Fiction / Romance / Romantic Comedy

Media City Publishers, Los Angeles
www.MediaCityPublishers.com

Cover Design: Jana Rade, Impact Studios
Edited by: Dr. Stephen K. Powell

Praise for Oprah Winfrey Hates my Guts

"I've been wondering who might fill the intellectual void that plagued me after James Baldwin died. Clearly it is Ta-Nehisi Coates. But this book filled some other kind of void and left me feeling some kind of way." ~ **Toni Morrison**

"It sent chills up my spine. Oooh, I like it." ~ El Debarge

"Of the writing of books, there is no end...but this is a good one. I encouraged Barack to try something like this for his next book—less seriousness, more levity."
~**Michelle Obama**

A note to readers

This story takes place in Chicago, in 2010. A time when Oprah Winfrey ruled the daytime television airwaves and shook global markets with every word she uttered. Her media power remains unmatched.

In the days of Egyptian, Greek and Roman mythology, a hero's success or failure was often attributed to whether or not a god or goddess favored that hero. In today's society, celebrities are the closest thing we have to the gods and goddesses of old. In some ways, we worship celebrity. If a celebrity agrees to be in a film, the film can be greenlit for production. If a celebrity endorses a product, people buy it. If a celebrity runs for president… You get the point. Oprah was/is the celebrity of celebrities—Zeus, if you will—atop Mount Olympus. At the time of our story, she was the celebrity maker, having only a few years earlier endorsed new and fairly unknown senator from Chicago, Barack Obama, for president. Clearly, Oprah's favor has led to unlimited success for many—just ask Dr. Phil, Dr. Oz, and countless authors, gurus, and artists. That's what happens when the goddess likes you, but imagine if she doesn't.

Although Oprah and other celebrities' names are used in this book, they will likely deny that any of this ever happened. And though it would be really cool if they all played along just for fun, this is a work of fiction. The author does not know or believe that Oprah actually hates anyone's guts. Nonetheless, it is conceivable that all of us, at some time or another, might believe that someone hates us based on various coincidental circumstances that might make such a conclusion feel reasonable—especially to a particularly troubled mind, such as our hero's. Moreover, this is a humorous work, a fun work, not meant as a criticism or interpretation of anyone's actions. That Oprah hates his guts is simply a belief of the main character at a time of crisis in his life, not a commentary on Ms. Winfrey's mind, heart or attitude.

The author chose to use Oprah's name because it is easier to understand the media power involved. Had another name been chosen, too much time would have been used up explaining who the person was while all the time trying to get people to think of Oprah. Moreover, "Susan Davenport (or any other name) Hates my Guts" does not really convey anything particularly frightening upon first hearing it. Besides, no one else who did a show in Chicago also owned a farm in Indiana.

Chapter One

Chicago, 2010

*T*he most wonderful time of the year had arrived and covered Chicago in all its seasonal, yuletide glory. Snow fell against bare elm trees, where it clung and reflected the millions of white, holiday lights hung way back in October. People bundled up against the winter chill made their way up and down the icy sidewalks lugging bags from Bloomingdale's, Marshall Field's and Nordstrom's, while the FAO Schwartz bear waved down at them from his sentinel position, congratulating them on maxing out their credit cards.

Misted breath from the nostrils of the Handsome Cab Horses blew little clouds into the night sky. The cappuccino and chocolate vendors hawked their hot beverages to the passing crowds to warm them against the icy wind that blew in from Lake Michigan to freeze the Magnificent Mile.

Above all the Michigan Avenue frivolity, lights from the twenty-sixth floor of the John Hancock Center shone inside, Ella Fitzgerald sung about sleigh bells jingling, ring-ting-ting-aling, too. The good folks at the Mitchell-Nagy Funds knew how to throw a party. The banner year of a hundred and twenty percent growth gave them good reason to celebrate. According to articles in the Wall Street journal, Fortune 500, and Business Week, Ronnie Mitchell was a money-making genius. He knew his way around the stock market like a preacher knows his Bible. When he had teamed up with Dana Nagy, a woman so no-nonsense and well-versed in bull and bear markets even Donald Trump once acknowledged her with a grunt, there was no stopping Mitchell-Nagy's accent to the top of the financial heap. And this year's holiday party was the cherry on their cake of a year.

These were precisely the thoughts of Ronnie Mitchell, the young entrepreneur who spearheaded the company, as he surveyed the sea of employees before him. He took a long, sophisticated sip from a flute of Dom Perignon, then raised his glass to his workforce. They elevated theirs in response to their beloved and wise leader.

"People as smart as Dana and I don't need help getting rich," Ronnie joked. "But when you do, it's important to remember all the little people. So we got you all a surprise."

Dana's champagne stopped halfway to her mouth. Ronnie did not mention anything to her before, and she detested spontaneity—unless it was very well-planned. "What surprise?" Dana whispered to him with a hushed suspicion. "You know I don't like surprises."

Ronnie winked at her and smiled. Paranoid Dana. It was sexy as hell and one of the reasons he loved her so much—she always worried about the little things. Ronnie gestured to the back of the room, where the rent-a-Santa he had hired appeared.

"Ho, ho, ho!" Santa proclaimed, as he made his way through the crowd, passing out golden envelopes from his green crushed velvet sack. Some of the recipients began tearing them open, but -

"Don't open them yet," Ronnie insisted. He did not want anyone to spoil the surprise. His employees were the reason for his success and this was just a small token of his great appreciation for all their hard work. He watched with joy as each received their envelope and waited patiently.

Dana's eyes narrowed at him. Her stare laser focused until the last envelope was distributed. *There'd better be Starbucks cards in those stupid envelopes*, Dana thought and nearly said out loud. Anything more than that and Ronnie would be spending the rest of the night wrestling one of her size ten Christian Louboutins out of his ass.

Ronnie glistened with anticipation. Four years had passed, during the worst economic collapse in his lifetime, during which the fund had been unable to show appreciation, but the promise of eventual success for all the hard work had finally paid off. He now had enough to share the way he always wanted. Ronnie had always been a generous man even before he was successful. He always appreciated people and treated them fairly. He had even sacrificed his own salary in order to continue employee benefits during the hard times. For him, the greatest joy of earning money was being able to give it away. Each and every gaze locked exclusively on him, waiting for permission and trembling with anticipation. Ronnie held on to that sensation until the last employee received her envelope—he placed his arm around Dana's waist and pulled her in closer. She would love this, too, he figured. It was, after all, from the both of them. But she would never let it pass her critical eye. She was far too conservative for this level of generosity, and Ronnie knew it. But what good was money if you couldn't share it? Besides, the write-off would come in handy for tax purposes. Dana could not deny that. Besides, it was only shares. It was not like anyone would sell them.

"Now!" he shouted.

They tore open the envelopes like children with presents on Christmas morning. A collective gasp filled the hushed room followed by a huge burst of laughter and screams of delight. Rose Patterson, the receptionist at the main desk yelled, "Hallelujah! Thank you, Jesus!" And even those with no particular religion seconded the exclamation.

Tears formed in Ronnie's eyes as he watched their reactions. He kissed Dana on the cheek. "They're so happy," he whispered to her. "Look how happy we made them." He turned to Dana anticipating her to be filled with the same joy he felt.

It wasn't there. Instead, her eyes burned holes through him. "What exactly is in those envelopes?" she demanded through a forced smile.

"Just a few shares of the fund." Ronnie twisted his face, confused by her reticent demeanor.

"How many shares, Ronnie?"

Ronnie smiled. "We had a crazy good year, boo. We can finally show them our appreciation."

"That's what their paycheck is for," she forced through a fake smile.

"We got a bonus, baby. We can share a little, can't we?" Ronnie reasoned.

"We built the company, Ronnie. Which one of these people were there when we were in your mom and dad's basement?" She waited for the answer she knew he could not give.

The energy sucked out of Ronnie, "I'm sorry,

baby. It's a write off though." He threw his last card out hoping it might help change her mind.

"How many shares, Ronnie?"

"Oh, my God, Mr. Mitchell, Ms. Nagy," Rose Patterson wiped a tear from her brown cheek, "eleven hundred shares? I can finally stop worrying about putting my daughter through college." Dana spit her champagne into a fine mist, then played it off as a coughing fit. "Oh, my God, Ms. Nagy, are you okay?"

"She's fine," Ronnie assured the woman. "You're more than welcome. We're glad we could help."

Rose hugged her bosses. Ronnie embraced the woman fully while Dana more or less accepted the invasion of her personal space. Numbers crunched through her mind in a mental, mathematical avalanche. Once the woman made her way back to the festivities, Dana was free to say what she really thought, "One hundred thousand dollars?" she hissed. "Are you out of your freaking mind? You gave every one of them one hundred thousand dollars?" She began counting the number of employees in the room even though she knew there were sixty-five exactly.

Ronnie downed the last of his drink and decided to leave Dana to brew in her own Grinchitude. He would enjoy the moment. He would enjoy being generous. He pointed to the happy cadre, "For those too drunk or too dumb to do the math – you're rich, bitches!" Cheers erupted like Mount Saint Helens. People hugged and kissed; tears of joy spilled from every orbital socket in the room. Ronnie poured the last of the Dom into his glass, and toasted his people again. "Now, you can quite buying those cheap-ass gifts for Boss' Day," he said. A wave of laughter rolled through the room.

Dana pinched the very sensitive flesh of Ronnie's underarm, squeezing it between her exquisite French manicure. Ronnie winced.

"The hell?" he said, jerking his arm away. "It's just money, Dana."

"It's impulsive! Outrageous!" Dana returned, working herself into more and more anger as the cortisol coursed through her body. "Irresponsible! Insane!"

"It's also too late," Ronnie said as he rubbed his arm. "Merry Christmas anyway." He leaned in for a kiss that was not there.

Dana looked at her shoe and considered exactly how much force it would take to require a proctologist to remove it. She changed her mind. Though possessed of almost supernatural self-control, she clenched her fists, bit her lip, and decided self-control be damned. The magnificent Mister Mitchel just threw away a significant portion of her own hard-earned money on a bunch of worker bees, and just as she was about to send one of her clenched fists into his oh-so-masculine jaw line, Donna from accounting stepped up to them. An enormous smile plastered across her face. She could barely speak through her emotion.

"Of course," Donna began, sniffling her way through her next sentence, "you know this means I'm quitting New Year's Day."

Ronnie got the joke immediately and laughed along with Donna. Dana wondered how against company protocol it would be to send left hooks into both of their faces. She would not get the chance, though. Donna and Rose had inadvertently spawned a tidal wave of gratitude amongst the Mitchell and Nagy personnel. They were surrounded by hugs, weeping, and mass appreciation. One of the IT guys, Jack Holland, Dana thought his name was, wrapped his arms around her in a crushing embrace. Jack was big as a grizzly and as hairy as one, too.

Dana feigned mutual affection despite Jack's big, wet tears of joy dripping against her neck and his sweaty armpits threatening her Salvatore Ferragamo blazer.

Merry Christmas, indeed.

* * *

The view from Ronnie's office was especially nice because his corner office windows butted against each other at the corner and gave a full one hundred and eighty degree view. He was actually in the middle of a meeting, but his mind was elsewhere. The two representatives from Bartlesby Finance were not part of his current equation. Bill Talbot and Harry Robinstone waited patiently, but their patience was running thin. They were two of Wall Street's top lawyers.

Bill leaned forward in the thick, leather chair Ronnie lavished on those who visited him in his office. "That's salary Ron," he said, pointing at Bartlesby's proposal. "It's a lot more than you make now. And on top of that, your bonus. A half percent of earnings."

"Last year that was ten million," Harry accentuated.

Ronnie's eyes bulged involuntarily, but he

fought the temptation.

Bill sighed. "Okay. We're authorized to raise the bonus to three quarters of a percent."

"That's fifteen million, Ron. Of course, you can do the math," said Harry, and waited for a response.

This time Ronnie bit his lip and kept quiet.

Bill and Harry exchanged a look. There was playing hardball, and there was just playing stupid. What was up with Mitchell? He didn't really think the silent treatment would work, did he?

"Fine," said Bill. "One percent. But that's the—"

"I appreciate Bartlesby's offer," Ronnie replied. "But I can't work for those blue suit assholes. I don't look good in blue." He turned around, his gaze going past the two men and straight to a lovingly framed picture of him and Dana in simpler times. They sat at two laptop computers, smiling for the camera, a pegboard of hand drawn stock charts behind them. "We started this company from scratch. In my parent's basement," Ronnie recalled. "Me and that chick right there."

Bill and Harry watched as Ronnie crossed the room, took the picture, and handed it to them.

"Our company would belly go up," Ronnie went on. "I'd ruin her. And I could never do that and live with myself or with her."

Ronnie smiled big, to himself, and produced a ring box from his pocket. He showed it to Harry.

"I'm asking her to marry me tonight," Ronnie said.

"Uh, congratulations, Ron, but –"

"Bill, Harry," Ron said in absolute and honest

openness, "I come from a labor family. My dad worked forty years in a steel mill. My sister, fifteen at the same office. My brother, fourteen for G.E. I broke that trend."

Harry was unimpressed with the Mitchell family history. For him, it was all about money—the more the better. He handed the picture to his partner and picked up the proposal. "It's twenty times what you make now."

Ronnie nodded. "My dad thought I was nuts when I started this company instead of taking a Wall Street job." He took a proud inhale. "My name is on this business. It means everything to me. It has to succeed. I want my employees to trust me and this company like my dad trusted Republic Steel."

Bill and Harry's disbelief grew as Ronnie crossed the room and opened the door.

"Thank Mister Norton for me, please." Ronnie said. "But no."

Harry shoved the proposal into his briefcase. He followed his partner out of the office. Bill paused at the door to return the picture to Ronnie. Before he did, he looked at it again. A spark ignited as he passed it to Harry. Harry grabbed to return it to Ronnie, but Bill did not let go. Instead, Bill waited for Harry to look up. Harry searched his partner's eyes—they moved down to the left side of the picture. Harry got it now. "Well, best of luck Ron. You're doing a great job here," Bill said as he exited the office. Harry handed the picture to Ronnie and left without a word.

Ronnie replaced the picture just so carefully on the shelf. He looked down at the engagement ring he still held in his hand, closed the lid, and placed it back in his pocket.

Down the hall, the elevator doors dinged open. Dana stepped out, her attention fixed on her armload of manila envelopes and legal pads. It was way too early to be this busy, and the cafe-latte-extra-shot-of-hazelnut espresso hadn't kicked in yet. Dana's decaffeination didn't sway her assistant, though. Jill Burns looked as if she'd been hooked up to an I.V. drip of dark roast all night.

"Good morning, Ms. Nagy!" Jill chirped, locked and loaded fingering her iPad and shuffling through a ream of papers on her arm. She didn't give Dana any time to reply as she handed her the first of the early morning documentation. "Your speech for tomorrow's luncheon," Jill said, then scrolled through her appointments. "Your ten forty-two is moved to ten fifty-one, as you requested. Your ten fifty seven is reset for eleven-o-nine. And, your mother is in recovery. Stable condition."

Dana stopped dead, her gaze transfixed on something in the distance.

Jill cleared her throat. "She had surgery today…"

"No, no," Dana said, and pointed to Bill and Harry, helping themselves to complimentary herbal tea in the reception room outside her office, "Why are Bartlesby's drones here?"

"They dropped by unexpectedly. They requested an appointment, but I told them you didn't have time today," Jill replied. "They asked if they could have some tea. I told them to help themselves." Dana continued staring a second.

Harry noticed her first. "Miss Nagy!" he called to her, "We'd love a minute of your time."

"I'm sorry sir," Jill interrupted, "I told you—"

"It's okay, Jill. One minute exactly, gentlemen," Dana said as she headed into her office, "speak quickly."

Moments later, Bill and Harry, each with their respective Earl Greys with lemon, sat in Dana's office sipping while Dana combed over their proposal with wide, unbelieving eyes.

"That's salary?" Dana queried.

"Not including the *one tenth* of one percent bonus," Harry responded, picking a bit of lemon from his teeth.

Dana stared out her window above Michigan Avenue. Though she didn't have the corner office, she had the better view up Michigan Avenue.

"So, last year I would have made an extra two million."

Bill consulted his calculator for verification, "Correct," he replied.

Dana shook her head. "But… this would ruin Mitchell-Nagy Funds."

"Dana," Harry began but seeing the look on Dana's face, changed his mind. "Ms. Nagy, you'd be the manager of the third largest mutual fund in the world. You buy, the market goes up. You sell; it goes down. It's real power."

Dana looked down at the proposal again, then to Bill and Harry. Over their blue-suited shoulders, her copy of the framed picture of her and Ronnie at old laptops in a garage smiled back at her.

* * *

Ronnie did his absolute damnedest to create the right atmosphere. Not too difficult a task, as his Lake Point Towers penthouse was prime for impressing. Imported Italian leather, matching credenza, and hand-stitched Moroccan suede pillows—it could have been on the cover of *Penthouse Beautiful*. Candles flickered over the romantic dinner Ronnie had catered, their flames reflecting off the pristine double-etched glass table imported from Napoli. He clinked his Waterford glass to Dana's and winked.

"We make one hell of a team, baby," he said, followed by a small sip. He smiled. She smiled back. He put down his glass, and regarded her for a moment. Dana had been quiet this evening which was unlike her.

"Da—"

"Ron—," They spoke simultaneously. Dana gave the floor.

"Dana, I've been doing some thinking." The ring box in his pocket seemed to grow heavier. He shifted slightly.

"Wow. Me, too," she replied, then laughed uncharacteristically. "Great minds, huh?" she said. She gestured for him to go on and downed the rest of her champagne.

"You're beautiful. You're brilliant. You're –"

"Bubbly?" Dana suggested.

"Funny," Ronnie said.

"Sorry. Thought it had to start with a "B". Go ahead."

"Dana—"

"No, don't," she took the floor this time. "Stop. Let me guess. It's another surprise?" she asked, trying not to appear as though she was gritting her teeth. "You love me?"

Ronnie was taken aback. He had everything rehearsed. He wasn't good on the fly, not where emotional matters were concerned. And the fact that Dana was yawning and not bothering to cover it up was a bit concerning.

"Before you drop to your knees, Ronnie, you should know the feeling's not mutual," she confessed matter-of-factly. "It may console you, however, that I entertained the thought once. For about six minutes. But…" She paused a beat as if thinking it through again before saying, "naaah."

Was she being serious? Ronnie couldn't tell. Dana had often played with his emotions during their time together. He was sure the that feeling was mutual and that she had gotten past the error of the other night, for which he'd apologized profusely and even offered to repay from his own salary over the next few years.

Dana folded her fingers together and leaned forward like a teacher about to tell a student why she gave him an F. "You're annoying, Ronnie. Childlike. I consider you silly for your age. You're a spoiled brat. I find none of that attractive."

"What?" The accusations came out the blue. She'd never said anything like it to him before. Dana had only ever admired Ronnie and told him so on many occasions. What was this?

"The main thing I admire about you is your ability to surround yourself with talented people who show you the way. For example, me."

Dana poured herself another glass. Ronnie grinned. He got it. She was playing with him. Okay, fine. Let her play. Like a cat and mouse. She can have her fun. "You *are* funny, Dana," Ronnie said. "You had me there. Got me all insecure and vulnerable."

"Oh, no…" she analyzed his response, "not denial." She shook her head pathetically. "Ronnie. I have plans for my life. Mitchell-Nagy is a stepping stone. It's like Oprah Winfrey says, 'I have to be the best me I can be'."

Ronnie's brows knitted together. She was quoting Oprah Winfrey? A talk show host? Since when did Dana watch Oprah? She must be joking. "You love me, Dana. You want to spend the rest of your life with me. You, me, our business. Our life. We talked about our dreams together." he reminded her. "You're fucking with me, right?" he smiled, hoping she would stop. The ring box began to feel like a brick in his pocket.

"There's something you're not getting here," Dana explained, without really explaining anything. This was turning out to be harder than she thought.

"Not getting? We're made for each other, Dana. All our good times?"

"Ronnie, think. Do I ever mix business with pleasure?"

"What about that night on my desk?"

Dana's lips pursed as she shook her head, "You couldn't concentrate on the data."

"I concentrated just fine on your data," Ronnie said, with a sly expression. Dana's expression, however, strongly suggested his coy-boy game wasn't going to play this time.

"It's always business, Ronnie. Never let your heart get in the way of business."

She was serious. Her cold as stone, take no prisoners face left no doubt. It was the same face she used in business meetings. Which this evening, as it turns out, had become.

"I should go," Dana said.

Dana took up her purse, kissed his cheek, and saw herself out.

The candle flickered again, this time from the breeze created by the shutting door. Ronnie reached into his pocket, removed the ring box and regarded it. Tears streamed down his face. Devastated. His heart smashed into a thousand puzzle pieces. He hyperventilated to try to control his emotion. It didn't work.

Hours later, Ronnie was still howling into his pillow aided by copious portions of Grey Goose and Hypnotic. By 1am, he had calmed down. By 2am, he got a second wind and bellowed again. By 4am he began to calm but found another reason to break down and more reasons to drown his feelings in alcohol. At 6am, he passed out.

The alarm clock buzzed a half-hour later, and continued for an hour completely unnoticed, before giving up. Next to his bed, a mountain of Kleenex had grown—the soggy Alps of the broken hearted. Ronnie laid, near comatose, alone in custom silk sheets he had made for the occasion of that evening. Next to the mountain of tissues, the ring box had fallen open. The five-carat engagement ring dislodged from its velvet chamber and rested on the carpeted floor next to his silenced cell phone. He'd already missed four calls.

By 8am, the number of missed calls had risen to thirty-two. Ronnie snored away. The house phone in the living room chirped repeatedly, but he couldn't hear it. He had moved it out of the bedroom and into the living room to ensure he and Dana would not be disturbed under any circumstances.

One o'clock rolled around and Ronnie stirred. Barely. 2pm, he turned over. At 3:30pm, he rose from the dead. He rubbed his eyes, the muck of his mouth feeling like a coat of paste, leaned over the bed, and saw the time on the clock.

"Shit," he said. The markets were closed now. That's what he got for falling in love —

No sense of time. No sense of anything. Except being dumped by an ungrateful business partner. That's all she was. A business partner. And, since the omnipotent Mzzz Nagy held no remorse or sentiment for him, well, two could play at that game. The Bartlesby boys had one dandy offer on his table. It would work for him financially as well as for his sweet revenge. The only demand was that they buy out Mitchell-Nagy instead of ruining them. He wouldn't let that happen to her even if he hated her now. He wouldn't let that happen to his employees. They deserved better. Bartlesby would buy out Mitchell-Nagy and maybe even give Dana a spot somewhere far away from him.

Still hungover, emotionally and otherwise, he jumped out of bed, punched the remote for the television, and headed to his custom walk-in closet to dig out the blue dress jacket he swore he'd never wear. He took his phone with him, ignored the 55 missed calls and hit Contacts. His eyes were still blurred and his head was heavy, but he knew he had Harry and Bill's number in there somewhere. Ah-hah! There it was. He hit Call.

He searched for his jacket as he waited for Bartlesby's headhunters to pick up. He crossed the room slipping into his pants as the voice from the CNN Business Desk lofted through the air.

"Again," the anchor said, "The top story: Fund Manager Dana Nagy interrupted her speech to the Chicago Board of Trade this morning to announce that she will take over running Bartlesby Select Capital, the nation's third largest fund. For more, we go to Joan Sykes."

Ronnie dropped his blue jacket and his jaw. He couldn't have just heard that. He just turned the news on for Chrissakes. He ran back into the bedroom and watched Joan Sykes have trouble with her earpiece. Behind Joan's shoulder was a gleaming picture of Dana, shaking hands with Mister Bartlesby himself.

A receptionist's voice came over Ronnie's phone. "Bartlesby Funds, how may I direct your call?"

"That bitch!" Ronnie screamed.

The receptionist disconnected.

Joan Sykes looked very seriously into the camera. "Jim, the markets reacted immediately, with Mitchell-Nagy shares dropping off nearly ninety-five percent."

Ronnie dropped the phone and ran to his computer. "No. No, no, no, no..."

"Co-founder, Ron Mitchell, has been unavailable for comment," Joan continued callously unaware of the co-founder's feelings, "But, it's unlikely Mitchell-Nagy can survive this devastating news."

The screen on Ronnie's computer confirmed Joan's report. Mitchell-Nagy Fund had gone from seventy-seven dollars per, to three bucks.

Ronnie sunk into his chair. It deflated under his weight.

* * *

The offices of Mitchell-Nagy Funds were silent. Except for the murmurs of the soon-to-be unemployed.

The elevator doors dinged open, and Ronnie zombied out in the crumpled blue suit.

Ronnie's assistant, Mark, ran up to him, offering a cup of coffee that spilled over the rim of his Mitchell and Nagy Funds ceramic mug. He and Dana made them on one of those on-line sites, when the company first showed signs of life. Ronnie batted it out of Mark's hand and into the wall.

"Where have you been?" Mark puzzled. "Everyone's been calling. We tried your cell—"

Ronnie didn't hear him. He shuffled into his office and stared at his imported African mahogany desk.

Mark stopped in the doorway. "We tried your house, your mom's. Everyone's worried sick about you! What's going on with Dana? Everything's crazy! We don't understand—"

SLAM! Was all the answer Ronnie gave his employees for the time being. Ronnie moved to his overstuffed leather chair. Why was everything he bought so expensive? He wondered how much it might fetch on Craig's List. The door clicked open. "Mark, I don't want to be disturbed!"

"It finally happened, huh?" a deep, booming voice replied. "Just like I told you it would."

Ronnie spun around. The heavyset man in his seventies closed the door behind himself and stood over Ronnie.

"Dad?" Ronnie whispered.

"My big toe been hurtin' all week. I should've called you and told you somethin' bad was gonna happen. You went bust, boy! Lost it all, didn't you?"

Ronnie shook his head, trying to clear the cobwebs. He squinted, rubbed, and looked up again. His father was still there. Still pissed.

"Gambling!" his dad admonished. "That's all this market is. It's a racket! You shoulda got a good job like I said. Lawd. Lawd… what is you gonna do?" His dad's Mississippi accent became more pronounced when he was agitated.

"I… I don't--"

"Can't tell you nuthin'. That's the problem. Bullheaded like ya mama. Mr. Know errthing. Mr. Yale University. Mr. Shit Don't Stank. I told you ya shit was gon stank one day. But I believed, boy. I believe in you. You convinced me 'gainst my better judgment. Lawd, I believed." Ronnie's father went on, pacing frantically, growing more and more concerned. "You were on the right path. Good school. But it got you all puffed up. Spoiled you. Got you thinking you could get that easy money. Lawd. Lawd. I seent it comin', Lawd," he yelled at the ceiling.

"Dad, go home. Quit worrying… I'm gonna be okay. I was—"

"Oh, GOD, I begged you never to let me see this day, Lawd, I said NEVER let me see it!" He yelled louder, paced more, paused, and then… clutched his chest. "Oh, shit!"

"Dad?" Ronnie asked, panicked. "Dad!"

Ronnie's father stiffened and crashed to the floor.

* * *

The elderly organist from House of Wills Funeral Home played *Take Me Out to the Ball Game*, as the family of Mister Ronald Mitchell Senior paid their last respects. A fitting tune, the organist mused, as her strong brown fingers ran through the melody that instructed the buying of peanuts and Cracker Jack. The late Mister Mitchell was a huge Cubs fan his widow Brenda Mitchell had told the undertaker during the arrangements. She was just happy they hadn't dressed him up in a Cubs uniform. The organist slowly segued into *I'll Be Seeing You in all the Old Familiar Places.* Brenda's fear of ghosts made her a bit uneasy with that one.

Linda and Ted Mitchell looked down at their father, peacefully gazing in his coffin. Linda reached down and fixed her father's lapel. Ronnie stood a few paces behind them.

"Well," Linda sighed and turned to Ronnie,

"You finally killed him."

Ted put a hand on her shoulder. "Stop it, Linda. Ronnie didn't mean to kill Dad."

Linda forced a smile. "He knew what he was doing. Poor Mom."

Brenda Mitchell sat across the parlor, receiving condolences. Her shiny, gray hair was done up big and proper; her linen handkerchief smooshed in her lap. She dabbed at her eyes.

Linda narrowed her gaze at her youngest brother. "He died penniless, thanks to you," she said, not exactly trying to keep her voice down. "He put all his money into your stupid fund."

"He what?" Ronnie didn't expect that. His father never liked the stock market, let alone putting anything into a fund.

"Don't pretend like you don't know," Linda hissed. "He found out his life savings had gone from two hundred thousand to ten thousand. Probably figured he'd better hurry up and die while he could still afford the funeral."

Ted wrung his hands around his own handkerchief and snuffled. "I just hate Momma's gonna be all alone. Neighborhood's not what it used to be. But she won't move in with me," he said through a long sniff. "I'm afraid for her."

"I can move in with her. Keep her safe. Keep her company," Ronnie said.

"You don't have to do th—Wait! Things that bad, Ronnie?" Linda queried with accusatory suspicion.

"I just need time to think. Get back on my feet," Ronnie returned. "I can help out around the house. Make sure mom's good."

* * *

Ronnie waited outside a door that read, *Bank President*. It opened and Victor Waits, a burly man of fifty, greeted him enthusiastically. "Ronnie Mitchell! Ready to get back in the game?"

"Vick, I've come to discuss my mom."

Moments later, Victor rocked back and forth on his pneumatic chair. It was one of those lumbar-support jobs. It looked like fish net and was uncomfortable as hell, but his chiropractor insisted.

"You got one of these things in your office, Ronnie?" Victor asked, sliding his hands up and down the hard equally uncomfortable plastic arm rests.

Ronnie shook his head. He hated being on this side of a desk.

"So what's up?" Victor asked, bringing his elbows behind his back and getting a satisfying crack for his efforts.

"Dad lost all his money with me," Ronnie said. "He left her without a dime. Hell, I'm down to a few bucks myself."

"Ah, Ronnie. You're good for it. You hit a hard time. We all do. You've made plenty of money for people you can –"

"No, Vick. Not yet."

Ronnie got up and began to pace, studying the wood paneling of Victor's office. Cheap, like a car dealership in the Midwest. But that's the way Victor liked it. Bank presidents could afford to be eccentric.

Ronnie let out a huge breath. "I just want to set something up for my mom. I sold everything, already. My cars, jewelry, the penthouse. I'm done. I've got five hundred thousand left, and I want it invested in a trust fund. For Mom."

Victor's eyes twinkled. Any amount over two-twenty five and he'd positively glisten. "We can do that."

"But I want it to look like Dad left it for her. Pay off the house. Send her a monthly check."

"Like our previous arrangement?"

Ronnie nodded. Victor smiled.

"Anything you say, Ron," he said and reached for one of his ballpoints. The kind that came twenty to a pack. *Waste not want not*, was Victor's motto.

Chapter Two

"**D**early beloved," the minister proclaimed. "We are gathered here today to join this man and this woman in holy matrimony…. Again." He cast his eyes at the couple before him. "Y'all gonna stick with it this time, right?"

Beverly Bunn-Jones-Bunn nodded, embarrassed. She did not need her minister to make her feel sheepish. Her family, gathered there behind her, was doing a great job of that. It started a few months ago when she announced that she and Mark were going to give holy matrimony another shot. Beverly's father, Elliott Bunn, had almost choked on his peas. At first he refused to walk her down the aisle. Blamed his sciatica. But, one puppy-eyed look from his daughter got him to reluctantly change his mind. Children must be allowed to make mistakes. God willing, one day they may actually learn from them.

The minister adjusted his glasses. "Do you, Beverly-Bunn-Jones-Bunn, take this man, Mark Jones, to be your lawfully married husband?

"Again?" said an unseen member of the congregation. Beverly guessed from the heavy drawl it was Cousin Mike. He was never one to respect ceremony. Especially this one.

"I, uh… yes," Beverly said. Perhaps a bit too

quietly.

"You sure, Sister Bunn?" the minister asked.

"Yes," Beverly returned and wondered if that slight tinge of doubt would be considered a sin.

"Do you, Mark Jones, take Beverly Bunn-Jones-Bunn to be your lawfully married wife?"

A group of people in the congregation snickered. Mark puffed up his chest until the buttons on his tux protested. "I do," he said.

"You may kiss the bride," said the minister, fighting with himself every inch of the way not to add another "again" again.

Mark lifted Beverly's veil and planted a big wet one against her lips. "Take two," he whispered to Beverly. She forced a smile.

"Ladies and gentlemen, may I present to you, Mister Mark Jones and Mrs. Beverly Bunn-Jones-Bunn-Jones."

The applause was less than enthusiastic. In fact, almost non-existent. As the *new* couple turned to those in attendance, Elliott rose from the pew and announced in a southern drawl that sounded somewhat like Hillbilly Bear, "We gon do tha 'ception at da Ol' Country Buffet. One ov'r on 87'mph and Cicero. I'ma pay for the first fiddy and dats it." He then mumbled something and added, "Ya heard?"

The guests rushed out of the church to secure their spots in line and left Beverly and Mark in the aisle behind them.

"Daddy!" Beverly protested.

"I'm a pay for you two, too." He mumbled something else, "Hurry up, doh. Ya already got pictures from da firs time." He mumbled again, "When he was yungr wit mo hair." He turned and walked out while saying something that sounded like, "Better lookin' then."

* * *

It was springtime. Ronnie chewed on his bottom lip as he knelt in his father's garden. He'd always hated dirt, so he thought. When he first moved back in with his mother, he found her staring out of the kitchen window to a big patch of nothing more than weeds and overgrowth.

Mrs. Mitchell had hoped that with the springtime, some of the flowers and vegetables would make a grand return. Alas, only dandelions and peppermint seemed up to the task.

Ronnie had just come from the grocery store when he saw her looking at the garden. She did that a lot. He figured she missed his dad. Ronnie missed him, too, and wished he could talk to him about his life now. His father was old school—hard work, sacrifice and patience. Ronnie was good on the first two. He'd always been able to focus on goals and achieve them through diligence. But he was low on patience. He was discouraged, and discouragement was foreign. Ronnie's dad had lived through discouragement—he'd fought in a war, been separated from his family, been laid off at the steel mill, and even endured a three year-long strike for better wages. Ronnie needed that wisdom now. But, despite his father surviving a war, he couldn't survive Ronnie's financial failure. What Ronnie lacked most was someone to impress. If his dad were still around, he would have something to prove. They say a man never knows who he truly is until he loses his father. Ronnie was mostly worried that he was a giant zero. "You alright, Mom?" he had asked her.

"I imagine I'll just let the garden grow over. I don't have your dad's green thumb," she said. It was a shame, really. Fresh organic tomatoes was one of those luxuries she'd taken for granted. "I'd monkey 'round and kill all the vegetables, anyway."

Mrs. Mitchell turned and glared at her son. He flashed back to his childhood and remembered what that look meant.

Now, only a few months later, Ronnie had become adept at dirt and fertilizer. He taught himself to lay out rows, seed them, and marked each section with a seed pack on a stake. He strung lines for beans. Even went so far as to put in a scarecrow for the birds and stepping stones. One of his father's windmills had broken. Ronnie was in the process of repairing it when a voice he didn't recognize spoke from a neighboring yard. "Yo," the voice said. "I likes how you got it laid out."

Ronnie glanced behind him. A man about his same age, skinny and a little shady looking, gave him a wink and a smile. "Keeps me busy," Ronnie answered, and went back to his hammering.

"You got the lima beans, the collard greens, the string beans, the corn ..." The man read Ronnie's face, "I'm Moe," he said. "I live back of you, there. I used to holla at yo daddy when he was out here, tendin' the back forty," he said, then laughed at his own joke. "You Ron, the baby, right?"

"That's me," Ron admitted.

Moe grinned, very toothy. "He sho loved his

baby boy. You the one with the business, right? He bragged about you all the time."

Ronnie's screwdriver slipped out of the windmill. His father never said he was proud of him.

Moe took a handful of seeds from his pocket. "Last year, your dad asked my uncle for these," he said.

"What are they?"

"Uh… Jamaican Greens. Your dad loved em. They don't like sun, though. Y'mind..? Moe asked as he took the liberty of sprinkling them behind the garage. Moe grinned again. "I'll check back in a few weeks and make sure they growin' right."

"But—"

"No problems, yo. I'll holla," Moe said as he made a fist and held it out to Ronnie.

Ronnie, more perplexed than annoyed, bumped his fist.

"By the way," Moe went on as he turned back to his house. "You gotta school me on them stocks one day. I been wantin' to get down wit that. Stay up, Ron Ron."

"O...kay," Ron Ron answered. He glanced down at the back of the garage and made a mental note to water whatever Neighbor Moe had just thrown back there. He found the screw and began again on the windmill.

* * *

Thud, thud, thud.
The nose was continuous. Unrelenting.
Thud, thud, thud.

And far, far too early for this time of day.

Mark Jones didn't care, though. It was never too early.

His feet pounded against the treadmill. He pushed the *Incline* button on the state-of-the-art machine. He was aiming at a new record. He cranked up the volume on his iPhone. He was getting into it now—chanting along to the motivation series he'd downloaded moments earlier, "Every day in every way, I am getting smarter and smarter. Every day in every way, I am growing richer and richer," his cadence continued.

Thud, thud, thud.

"People like me. People love me! I... Am... So... Cool... YES!"

Thud, thud, thud.

Beverly stirred underneath the covers. She was dreaming of sledgehammers. Even as she slept, she found this stupid. Why would she be dreaming of sledgehammers?

"People love me. People love me! I. Am. So! Cool. YES!"

Not only was the sledgehammer annoying, it was narcissistic, too. In that groggy state between sleep and awake, Beverly reached out to shut the thing up. Her hand wrapped around the sledgehammer's handle – which, in reality, was a heavy candlestick given as a romantic wedding present for those special nights when the right light made all the difference in the world. They had not used it yet.

Beverly hurled the sledgehammer/candlestick away from her dream.

It hit Mark and his motivational speaker in the

back of the head. Mark fell on his ass, treadmill at
full speed, and flipped over backwards – a somersault
worthy of a nine point three. He managed to get to
his feet, but one of Newton's laws had something to
say about that. Arms flailing, he tried to catch
himself. No dice. He stumbled backward, straight
out the balcony door, over the railing, and into the
complex's pool.

Beverly let out a satisfied sigh as the
sledgehammer stopped sledgehammering. She
embraced her pillow, and buried her face against it.
This time, instead of thumping sledgehammers, she
dreamt of blossoming sunflowers. They were quiet.
So nice. And quiet.

Suddenly, one of the sunflowers started
screaming.

"What the hell is wrong with you?"

Beverly bolted upright, clutching the sheets to
her chest.

"You're trying to kill me?" yelled Mark. He
was soaking wet, standing in front of their bed with
his wet gym shorts stuck to his man parts like plastic
wrap.

"What are you talking about?" Beverly said,
grasping the sheets closer. "Did you go swimming?"
she asked.

"You tried to kill me!" Mark shrieked.

"No, I didn't! You're dreaming. Go back to
sleep."

"You call this a dream?" Mark admonished,
pointing to his soggy shorts.

Beverly clamored out of bed. "You must've
been sleepwalking. Did you get in the shower by
mistake?"

Mark's eyes narrowed. "I fell in the pool."

"Oh, baby! The pool?" Beverly empathized. "You okay? Wow. Why'd you go downstairs?"

Mark smoldered beneath his anger. "I…fell…off…the…balcony!" He enunciated each word slowly in between the deep breathes he took to calm himself down.

Beverly jumped and ran to the balcony railing. "My god, Mark, are you okay? Maybe we should move to a lower floor if you're sleepwalking now."

Mark seethed, "Sleepwalking? Are you crazy? No, you hit me in the head with a candle."

"Oh my god, you're hallucinating. Maybe we should get you to a hospital."

Mark couldn't believe it. Mark, breathing heavily, moved closer to her. He wasn't sure what he was going to do, but he wanted her to admit what she did. That was always the problem with Beverly, he thought. She never admitted her fault in anything. "You know you do this stuff all the time. You're always starting stuff and then acting like you had nothing to do with it. I'm going to leave you again if you can't admit when you're wrong."

"Admit what? I was sleep until you came in here screaming at me."

"I knew I shouldn't have married you! Again!"

"Mark, stop it! You're scaring me!" Beverly shouted. "Have you started drinking? I didn't know you started drinking. I don't think you should drink this early in the morning."

Mark seethed more as he moved in on her. "You still deny it?" He pointed to the candle wax weapon on the floor. "There it is! That one! It's probably got my blood on it."

"Baby," she said, completely disbelieving his story, "it's just the liquor talking. Go back to bed 'til you sober up. You'll be better soon."

"OH MY GOD!" Mark bellowed, as he began to pace, unable to take it any longer.

Beverly jolted upright like a squirrel seeing a dog—ready to head for the nearest tree. He was too close to her, now. Beverly faked a left, then spun right, and made a bee line for the door.

Mark stood there, ear buds dangling, water dripping. His iPhone remarkably still working. "Every day in every way, I am getting *wetter* and *wetter*," the guru reminded him.

* * *

By late June, Ronnie's garden was in full bloom. Particularly Moe's "Jamaican Greens," which, about a month ago, Ronnie realized was marijuana. Ronnie attempted to pull up the contraband, but Moe convinced him to leave it be. "The garage hides it, my man," Moe had said. Besides, "Yo, this go with er'thang." This was Chicago, so it always surprised Ronnie how many people here had southern accents. "It's a good tea. Good in salad."

"Tea?" Ronnie had asked. Really?" Ronnie couldn't resist and cut a few leaves to let steep in hot water while his mother took her afternoon nap. Ronnie left to use the bathroom and left the sauce pan unattended. To Ronnie's complete shock, his mother had awakened, noticed the steeping leaves, assumed they were peppermint and poured herself a cup of the most delicious tea she'd ever drank. Now, she wanted it every afternoon and often asked Ronnie to join her for "high tea," as she jokingly, unintentionally called it, quite ironically. Ronnie's days were now broken up by the productive time he had in the mornings and the complete uselessness of his post-tea afternoons with his mom. Most days they ended up vegging out on *Three Stooges* and *Honeymooners* reruns.

Moe helped himself to the leaves for many other purposes, but Ronnie limited his indulgence to high tea with his mom. The best part was that Ronnie's mom no longer seemed depressed about her husband's passing. For her, the tea sparked a new excitement about life. She'd taken up dancing classes in the evening and going to the gym in the morning. Ronnie didn't have the heart to tell her it was weed that had changed her life. She would have never been able to return to her church with that on her conscious. Instead, he simply enjoyed her being happy. Little did he know, it was a huge mistake.

Mrs. Mitchell's new found zest for life left her exhausted on Sunday mornings, and she had missed her fifth service in a row. Pastor Williams decided to pay the grieving widow a visit to determine if she needed help. Unfortunately for Ronnie, Pastor Williams was not only nosey but also had once been a weed man in the Cabrini Green projects where he grew up. Pastor Williams knew weed when he saw it, and he knew it when he tasted it in the tea Mrs. Mitchell had prepared for him.

"Oh, I thought you were grieving, but you up in here with the devil," her pastor told her as he quickly swallowed the rest of the tea, nearly burning his mouth in the process.

"The devil?" Mrs. Mitchell was shocked and appalled. She'd never had her uprightness questioned before and she wasn't about to start now. "I miss church a few weeks, and now I'm up with the devil? I think that's a little harsh, Pastor Williams."

"It may be harsh, sister," Pastor Williams licked his lips, "but do you deny you just gave a recovering addict a cup of cannabis tea?"

"Cannabis?! Is that what's it's called? It seems I've heard that word before, but I can't remember where I heard it. We grow these tea leaves in our own garden."

"You do?!" the pastor asked more excited than surprised. "Show me where."

Mrs. Mitchell led Pastor Williams out the back door and into the rear yard behind the garage. "They don't like too much sunshine, according to my son. We keep them back here so they get some shade."

Rev. Williams' eyes bulged at the sight of the magnificent bounty. Flashbacks of bygone days flooded his mind and drew a slight smile across his face. "Uh, Sister Mitchell, you know what this stuff is, don't you?"

"You said it was cannabis. That's some type of Jamaican herbal tea leaf, right?"

Pastor Williams waited, as if he expected his parishioner to confess. Mrs. Mitchell stared back innocently. "It's weed!" Rev. Williams finally made it plain. "Marijuana!"

"Marijuana?!" Mrs. Mitchell nearly fainted.

Pastor Williams steadied her until she found her legs again; he picked a few leaves, rubbed them between his palms to warm and express their essence, then deeply inhaled their pungency. He was instantly transported to heaven. *Oh that's some good shit*, he almost said out loud. "Oh, that's marijuana for sure," he said instead.

Sister Mitchell was beside herself with embarrassment. She clutched her face in her hands and turned away in shame.

Pastor Williams used the moment to secure a few branches of the herb and shove them into his jacket pockets. "You're saying you didn't know what this was, Sister Mitchell?" he questioned over his shoulder as he stealthily harvested some of the choicest bhang.

"I swear 'fore God, pastor, I had no idea. Ronnie bought it in here and made me some tea with it and…," she considered the number of times she'd had high tea with Ronnie and wondered if he knew all along. "We had high tea."

"High tea?" Pastor Williams questioned. "That didn't give it away?" Mrs. Mitchell sat on the edge of a chaise lounge and tried to collect her thoughts. "So you've been missing church because you've been too busy getting high with your son?"

"No!" she gasped. "I was just tired."

"Well, that's what marijuana will do to you."

"No, not from that—from exercising every day and dancing every night."

"Dancing? You started clubbin' now, too, uh? Just getting high and clubbin'. Ronnie got you doing all the devil's pastimes." Reverend Williams' stern eyes burned guilt right into Brenda Mitchell's heart. She repented right there in the garden and turned her life back over to Jesus before it was "too late."

When they had finished praying, Mrs. Mitchell determined to have Ronnie rip the plants up right away, but Reverend Williams cautioned her not to push Ronnie if he wasn't ready. The good reverend himself would set an appointment to visit Ronnie regularly to help him find his way back to Jesus. Mrs. Mitchell thanked Pastor Williams and bid him farewell. He left, pockets stuffed with Mary Jane, as he called it in his day.

Two days later, Pastor Buck Williams visited Ronnie Mitchell while Brenda Mitchell was at the gym. The following Sunday, Buck missed church. The next Tuesday he was seen at Ronnie's house again, this time during Sister Mitchell's dance class. Buck missed Bible Study on Wednesday and neglected to inform his assistant pastor. After he missed the following Sunday, the deacon board dispatched a team to investigate the matter. They activated the tracking app in the pastor's phone and found ol Buck Williams down at Lake Michigan with Ronnie, fishing and toking blunts.

Before he met Buck Williams, Ronnie had only tried smoking weed once in college. He hadn't liked it. It interfered too much with his concentration. For the most part, an occasional glass of wine was as far as he would allow himself to go in school. Once he graduated he drank only on special occasions and usually either champagne or a shot of vodka. The tea had been a relaxing departure from the stress of his recent failure, but it was a mild high compared to the punch of inhaling the smoke directly. The pastor had another convert.

The deacons reported their findings to the rest of the board. Buck Williams was terminated posthaste.

* * *

The afternoon aqua-aerobics class was in full, no-impact swing, or splash, as the case may be.

Beverly had signed herself up, along with childhood friends Shenique and Denise, in an effort to keep her mind off of her next impending divorce.

Shenique panted heavily, her buxom chest heaving up and down, in time to the music. "That's right, you keep it Beverly-Bunn-Jones-Bunn-Jones-Bunn. Remind your ass how stupid you are."

Beverly ignored her.

"You're not stupid, Bev," Denise said, trying to be sympathetic. She wiped a stray lock of hair from her face. Then another. "You just… love hard."

Shenique threw Denise a contemptuous look. Denise shrugged. "There's nothing wrong with giving love a second chance, Shenique."

"No, but there is something wrong with marrying the same dude twice."

"I don't know what I was thinking," Beverly said.

"You weren't thinking," Shenique snickered. "You never do. You're a sucker for love."

"Better a sucker for love," Denise tried to defend her friend, "than a lover of… suck." It had made sense in her mind before she heard herself say it. At least she tried. Beverly patted her on the back to let her know she understood the meaning behind the senseless words.

Shenique gave Denise a look, then splashed her. "You know what you need, Beverly Bunn Bunn?" Shenique suggested. "Some Oprah Winfrey. She'll help you be the best you can be."

Beverly exhaled and submerged herself. She sat cross legged at the bottom of the pool like a brick, and she liked it. *Maybe this is the best I can be*, she thought.

* * *

Three months after Ronnie first met his buddy Buck, he lost all interest in growing anything else. Gone were the organic tomatoes, the corn, the carrots, celery and beans—all overgrown by Moe's greens.

Inside the home, muffled hip-hop filtered up from the basement. Mostly, it was a steady deep beat. Mrs. Mitchell had had enough. She wrestled a Windex bottle from beneath the kitchen sink and stormed off to her living room. Along the wall photographs hung like a family tree. At the top, Mrs. Mitchell and Ronald Senior hugged on their wedding day. Beneath them, their three children: Ted, Linda and Ronnie. Beneath each child, a series of photo highlights showed their history. Ted and Linda had pictures of their marriages—Ted's wife, Freda, in her white, poufy dress and café au lait skin. Linda coupled up with her husband, Jeff, the white boy she'd bought home from college as a surprise that nearly killed her father years ago. Beneath each couple, their children.

By contrast, Ronnie's pictures began with his B.A. Degree from Yale, dated 2005. The rest of his photos were of his epic achievements in the business world: newspaper clippings, magazine covers and articles—a *Business World* and *Black Entrepreneur* magazine feature. And the highest prize—an Ebony magazine cover story featuring a picture of Ronnie and someone familiar with a crown drawn on her head, a cigar drawn in her mouth, evil, arched eyebrows scribbled across her head and a thought bubble that read, *Heh, heh, sucker!* Across her business jacket, angrier block letters were scribbled which read *User* and *Liar*.

Mrs. Mitchell spritzed the photo with the Windex and waited for the ammonia D to do its work. Slowly, the hand-drawn ink melted grotesquely down the glass. She wiped it away revealing a smiling Dana Nagy beneath Ronnie's protective arm. "Til I get on my feet," she said under her breath, deeply troubled by what her son had become. "He took the pastor down, but he's not going to take me down." She shook her head and exhaled a frustrated "Umph." She carefully replaced the picture on the wall. "Well," she said to herself, "it all ends today."

In the basement, Ronnie had set up camp. The music from the TV blasted loudly enough to vibrate the kitchen door. A sexy woman's voice accentuated the beat with the moaned lyric, *Ooh, baby, ooh, ooh.* It was the latest hit from the Babylon Sisters—a nasty trio of women who, despite the inability to sing, seemed to be doing fine in the music business.

"Yeah, you say you want me…. User! I'm on to you… First, you go zzurppp, then you go pppffft." The words came from a barely coherent mass laying across an old cream and brown sofa that once decorated the Mitchell's living room. Ronnie had gone to pot… literally. He still maintained a scruffy handsomeness, but he was a shadow of his former self. He peeked through half-squinted, bloodshot eyes to confirm his prediction.

On the TV, the video for the song played. The Babylon Sisters danced and pranced during the chorus, which featured the sound effect Ronnie had made. The *Zzurppp* was the sound of the middle singer unzipping the front of her leather bodice. The *Pppffft* was the sound of her breast falling out and bouncing behind a blurry spot. Ronnie's eyes followed the bouncing ball.

"Yeah, that's how you all do it. You're after me lucky charms," Ronnie continued droning to himself, "You'll never get em again you USERS!" He barked half-incoherent at the screen, "Look at you. Shame! YOU. DON'T. LOVE. ME!" He slurped his tea and molded back into the sofa. Despite having smoked an entire blunt in the garage earlier, he never dared to smoke in his mother's home no matter how high he was. Empty tea cups surrounded him. He continued watching the Babylon Sisters shake it, then he rolled forward, grabbed a dart off the coffee table and flung it. It stuck hard in the middle of a *Business Week* cover photo of Dana on the wall, right next to three previously thrown darts. The cover read, *Bartlesby Soars Under New Management*. "Yeah!" Ronnie barked at the screen again, "All hail Dana. The mother of users. BOW DOWN!"

The Babylon Sisters bowed their heads, as if on cue, as part of their dance. Ronnie was familiar with the choreography as well. Then came the good part—the part that made him furious with rage. The sister on the left stepped forward from the rest of the group and started rapping, "*I'm so hot, my ice dripping, baby. I got that mad luchie like Dana Nagy.*"

"THAT SHIT DOESN'T EVEN RHYME!" Ronnie raged. "How is this rap? BABY—NAGY? What is the world coming to? UGH! And you CAN'T SING EITHER! WHY ARE YOU ON TV?!" The sisters continued dancing and rapping and driving Ronnie further out of his mind. A doorbell rang upstairs, but Ronnie didn't hear it. Instead, he brewed like tea leaves, in the funky heat of burning betrayal, jealousy and rage.

Mrs. Mitchell opened her front door to three huge men in black military camouflage with patches on their pockets on which were printed the initials *B.B.G./M.A.* The muffled drum of the music vibrated beneath their feet as they entered. "So nice to meet you," she said. "When I saw you on TV, I knew you were just what I needed."

Behind the men, in the driveway, their van identified their specialty: A cartoon painting of a large brown hand grabbing a saggy pants man, mid toke on a joint. Stenciled beneath in large Black letters: *Boy-B-Gone and Man Away.* This was followed in italics by the explanatory motto, *We Take Your Grown Man Off Your Hands.* The first man, the smallest of the three, still easily six foot two, a deuce and a quarter of Alabama country strong, handed her a clipboard, "Please sign on the dotted line. Warranty's good for one year," he said.

Mrs. Mitchell took a moment, a very, very brief moment, then scribbled her name on the bottom of the form and passed it back.

"In the basement," she said.

"Like most of 'em," he replied before opening the basement door and clicking on a flashlight. "Now tell us, does he have any martial arts training? We don't wanna get down there and find we've got a MMA enthusiast on our hands."

"No. Ronnie's a tall man, but he wouldn't hurt a fly." She thought about it some more. "You will be gentle with him, won't you? I don't want him hurt."

"We'll be gentle ma'am—as long as he he's gentle. It's best if you just go to the living room. We'll let you know when we're done."

Mrs. Mitchell walked away reluctantly. The men moved down the stairs pouring fluid into a rag.

Ronnie took a long sip of tea and sang the chorus with the Babylon Sisters, slowly torturing himself, "*Mad luchie like Dana Nagy*! I know. YOU EVIL BIT—"

The word stuck behind the cloth that now covered his face. Ronnie's reflexes took a second to respond. First his eyes bulged, then a muted scream, then he tried to jump up, but suddenly weighed 500 pounds as the two larger men pinned his shoulders to the couch. Full panic mode took over, as he swung blindly at the demon that had attacked him, then threw his foot over his head and connected squarely on the jaw of the largest of the men. The goliath released his grip, grabbed the side of his face, and then hit the floor. The smallest man sat on Ronnie's legs and held them down until the drug took effect.

It wasn't long. Ten seconds later, Ronnie was sleep.

* * *

The motel was rated half a star on Yelp—multiple complaints about poor management, hookers, and occasional rapes. The view from the window was filmy, allowing the occupant a stellar vista of a broken air conditioning unit. A shaft of afternoon sun broke through, dust mites and god-knows-what illuminated in the ray of light.

Ronnie stirred and woke slowly. His head felt like a heavy cotton ball, and his mouth tasted of day-old Doritos. He sat up, the comforter of the bed crackling as he did so, and tried to focus on where the hell he was and how he got there. He was about to rationalize it as the consequence of a blackout, when something caught his eye. Expertly taped to the television was an official looking envelope with the initials *B.B.G./M.A.*

It was difficult to pull himself up off the bed, but he managed somehow, though his legs felt like rubber. Ronnie took the paper from the television, and read it out loud, "*You have been evicted. The loved one you resided with determined that it was time for you to go. The rent on this room is paid until week's end.*" Ronnie shook his head to try and clear it. It didn't help. He steadied himself and continued; "*Do not attempt to return to your former dwelling as it is secured and under surveillance.*"

Surveillance? Ronnie thought. "What the fu—?" He continued reading, "Your belongings are in the closet. Enclosed please find a complimentary fifty dollars to ease your adjustment. Good luck."

He checked the envelope; there were four crisp new tens and ten ones. "Fifty dollars?!"

Ronnie took a minute to collect his thoughts and take in his new environs. They spared every expense—Motel 6 was the Four Seasons next to this joint. He checked the closet. There were two garbage bags of clothes. "This is bullshit!" he screamed while kicking one of the bags, which split open and spilled his clothes on the filthy carpet. "I own that house!" He began to weep and collapsed in a heap on the floor, pulling his clothes to his bosom. He looked up at the ceiling and wailed, "Et tu, Mama?"

Ronnie grabbed the remote. Or, tried to. It was leashed to the nightstand like a bad dog. He pushed the power button. Oprah Winfrey's face was plastered on the screen. Big, smiling, and perfectly maintained.

Ronnie snarled, resenting anyone who had the nerve to be happy when he was so miserable.

Oprah turned to her guest and smiled even wider as if she'd never met someone so impressive. "You've accomplished so much, and you're so young!" Oprah complimented. "I really admire you."

"Oh, I could never have done it without you," the guest replied. "You're my inspiration."

Ronnie slow burned as his former partner and Oprah exchanged a tap on the back and near-cheek kisses. Oprah held Dana away from her, as a proud mother does to the golden child.

"That is so sweet," Oprah said, then whispered into Dana's ear, "Watch the make-up, hon." Dana nodded, and beamed right back at her. "Two things that I just can't stand. Messed up make-up and..." she turned to the audience, "And...?"

"Cell phones!" the audience screamed.

"Oh, I get livid. I can't stand them." Oprah

grinned and blew her audience a kiss. Dana did the same.

That was all Ronnie could stand. His eyes darted back and forth as the fury built. He grabbed the old-school tube TV and tried to lift it, but it was bolted to the dresser. It didn't matter. He engaged more of his hulk-like fury and lifted the whole dresser, but he was either not that mad or not that strong. He dropped it and collapsed on the bed. Dana's face smiled and waved at him.

"You were nothing before you met me! NOTHING!" Ronnie shouted. "You USER! Liar!"

Again, Dana waved, then gave him a curt little wink.

"UGH!!!" He reached for the ice bucket to put it through the TV screen just as the show went to commercial.

The screen came up on a familiar face, "Hi, do you have a boy or even a grown man who won't take responsibility for his life and chooses instead to live off your kindness? We can help you. We're Boy-B-Gone and Man Away." The van drives past. "We take your man off your hands!" There's footage, which must have been filmed the previous day, of the van in front of Ronnie's house and Ronnie being dragged out the house. Mrs. Mitchell smiles for the camera and reads off a card, "My boy was so bad, he led our pastor astray, but thanks to Man-Away, our new pastor is safe." Mrs. Mitchell's new pastor steps forward, he looks familiar too, it's Moe, "Man-Away is a great service we recommend to women at the church who can't control their grown sons." The first man comes back on camera, "Ask about our same day service. Special discounts for viewers of the Oprah

Winfrey Show."

Ronnie was gobsmacked.

Next Oprah's face appeared, "I love these guys. So many of my viewers have called since I had them on my show and told me how much better their lives have been since they used Man Away. Give them a try today. If you're not fully satisfied with their service, I'll refund you your money personally. How's that for a guarantee?"

Ronnie shut off the TV and watched his haggard reflection stare back at him from the black screen.

* * *

The northeast wall of Beverly's three-bedroom Hyde Park high-rise was lined with exquisite black and white photographs—the kind you'd find in a posh art gallery. Each one displayed an image of various Chicago landmarks – Millennium Park, the Willis Tower, and Giordano's Pizza in Hyde Park among them. Each one was hand-signed, *Beverly Bunn*. Or *Beverly Bunn-Jones*. Or *Beverly Bunn-Jones-Bunn*, etc.

Beverly sat at her desk, her phone cradled under her chin, a small framed memento of her and Mark's second wedding in her hand. A flat-screen television droned on behind her, broadcasting the last of Oprah's Dana Nagy segment.

"I don't know," Beverly said to her unknown caller. "You think I should?... I mean, it seems too soon... Yeah, I know it's been three months... No I guess he's not..."

Beverly stood up and wandered over to the flat screen. The attractive business woman was giving Oprah a farewell peck on the cheek. As Dana left the stage, Oprah turned to the camera; her face became very serious. Stoic.

"Remember," Oprah said. "Put the past behind. Be decisive. That's just what Dana Nagy did, and look at her now!"

The audience cheered.

Beverly listened to the sound of the applause. Someday, people might cheer for her, too, if she was capable of making the right decision. She looked at her wedding photo, then placed it face-down on her coffee table—right next to an American Bride magazine.

"Okay," Beverly said to her phone. "I've made up my mind. I'll meet you guys there."

The voice on the other end screamed excitedly. Beverly held the phone away from her, wincing.

* * *

Ted Mitchell's suburban home was Norman Rockwell perfect. Picket fence, trimmed yard, Mercedes in the garage and a brand new hybrid SUV in the driveway. The back hatch of which was open and filled with camping equipment.

Ronnie and Ted loaded the last of the luggage into the SUV. Ted looked at Ronnie suspiciously. A dog barked at the end of the drive way. Misty, Ted's fluffy white cat, leaped into the cargo bay and hissed. "Hey there, girl; that mean old dog scared you again? It's okay. You're safe." Ted stroked the cat and it purred. "Yes, we're gonna miss you too." Ted got second thoughts. "Maybe we should wait until we're back."

"The fumes, the mess—this is perfect. I'll get the painting done and you don't have to worry about the kids breathing that crap. It'll be aired out when you get back."

"Look, Ronnie, I know mom kicked you out of the house."

"I bet you do," Ronnie's eyes cut right through Ted's soul.

"What's that supposed to mean?"

"'Time for little Ron to get back on his feet. You're enabling him, mom,' right?"

"A little bit."

Ronnie laughed then snarled, "Don't think I'm not aware of your global conspiracy to ruin my life. You put her up to it—that Man Away bullshit—that's classic you."

"It *is* time you got back on your feet, Ron. By the way, it was Oprah that convinced her to throw you out, not me," Ted insisted.

Ronnie gritted his teeth. "Put your money where your mouth is for once, Ted. Give me this job. Help baby brother get back on his feet."

Ted shook his head in resignation. Maybe he was an enabler, too. But family was family, and family came first.

"I left a few signed checks in the drawer," he said.

Ronnie's face lit up—this was going to be

easier than he thought. "The one under the cutting board in the kitchen?"

"Uh-huh," Ted returned, suspiciously. "It's only costing four grand, Ronnie. Four grand, that's it. You're not going to jack the price because you need more primer or better paint."

"Don't have to insult me, asshole."

"Or real linen drop cloths, or because you had to rent scaffolding?"

Ronnie patted Ted on the head. "You guys have a great trip, and we'll see you in two weeks. Everything'll be fine."

Ted reluctantly handed a set of keys to his little brother then took a quick glance into the garage.

"I know the mileage on that," he said and nodded towards his Mercedes E Class in the other space. "You can use it, but be careful."

"Be careful?" Ronnie shook his head at Ted, "What, no donuts or drag racing?"

"And don't forget to feed the cat." Ted handed Misty to Ronnie. Ronnie was a dog person. He tossed the cat in the garage.

Later that day, the odometer on Ted's SUV rolled to ten thousand miles. The couple's two boys, five and seven, sat in the back seat with headphones on and played video games on the flip-down screen.

Freda had been staring at Ted since they left the house. Ted finally ran out of other things to look at and occupy himself. He already knew the issue, "If it weren't for Ronnie—"

"I know. We wouldn't have that house. But that was a different Ronnie, Ted."

"Relax, babe, okay?" Ted said. "You know I'm no good at do-it-yourself projects, but Ronnie is. Just look what he did for dad's garden."

"Mm-hmm," she returned flatly.

"And if it wasn't for him—"

"You wouldn't have your job. Again, I know. And again, that was a different time, and that was a different Ronnie." Freda cast her gaze out the tinted window, watching the tree-lined highway pass before her. "Face it, Ted. Your brother's become a bum!"

"He's not a bum," Ted defended.

"Maybe it had to do with your dad passing away. Or Dana," Freda thought aloud. "What makes people become bums, Ted?"

Ted's fingers gripped the leather wheel a little tighter. "He's not a bum! He... he's just been through a lot."

"You're going to go through a lot if he screws up my house," Freda retorted. And turned again to watch the passing trees.

* * *

"....Nine and one, two, three, four, five, six, seven, eight, nine... Ten thousand dollars," the teller tallied as she lay the bills on the counter.

"Thank you," Ronnie said, and gave her a wink.

She smiled and winked back at him.

Ronnie still had it.

Chapter Three

Ronnie checked his reflection and liked what he saw. He cleaned up well. He looked ready for Wall Street. The haircut, manicure, shave, and new clothes worked on him. Damn, did they work on him. He secured a wad of big, big bills into a silver clip shaped like a dollar sign and slipped Ted's Rolex onto his wrist.

"Alright, boy," he said to himself. "You know you can't live here, and you damn sure can't stay at that motel. You could get a job, but that's how the suckers do it, right? And, who's going to hire you after such a public failure? Fuck it. You've been taking care of other people your whole life, and what did they do for you in return? Nothing. Threw you out on your ass the first chance they got. Okay." His reflection nodded in agreement. "And, you're never going to be a sucker again, are you?" Ronnie's reflection shook its head. "Time to do unto others as they have done unto you." Ronnie's reflection flashed a winning smile.

The Classified Section of the *Chicago Tribune* lay open on the kitchen counter. Ronnie leaned over it and began to study.

According to the want ads: an Office Manager, twelve fifty an hour; an engineer, thirty five; dental Assistant, forty-five K a year. A vice president of marketing held the most promise at a substantial six figures.

Ronnie was soaking in all of this when he felt something rub up against his leg. He jumped.

Ted's cat, Misty, rubbed a blob of hair into Ronnie's new pants legs, looked up at him, and meowed.

"Really?!" Ronnie exclaimed, brushing off the fur. Misty let out a low, rumbling growl. He shooed the cat into the laundry room with her litter box and shut the door. In the kitchen, he opened a bag of meow mix, filled a bowl, and shoved it into the laundry room along with a roasting pan full of water. He thought a second and decided to leave the rest of the bag of food in the laundry room, too. He dumped extra litter in her box and double checked the room, "You good?" he asked the cat. She purred. "Okay, see you later."

* * *

Buddy Guy's Legends was the only original blues club left in the city, and the place where Denise and Shenique determined to celebrate Beverly's personal Independence Day—men who chose blues over Babylon Sisters were sophisticated, Shenique reasoned. Less chance of running into immature boys there.

The party crowd bumped-and-grinded to five and twelve bar blues. Shenique looked over the rim of her piña colada to Beverly before doing her impression of her cousin, Peaches Monroee, "We in dis bitch, finna get crunk." Shenique smoothed her finger over her brows, "Eyebrows on fleek, da fuq."

Beverly screamed laughing. Shenique was her girl and knew how to lighten her mood.

"There you go. Loosen up," Shenique said and handed her coco-nutty beverage to Beverly.

Beverly took a sip.

Denise stabbed a maraschino cherry with a plastic sword and stuck it in her mouth, stem facing outward. She looked across the dance floor, wondering just when-oh-when the real men Shenique talked about were going to show up. So far, there'd been just one. The guy over by the bar, looking as though he'd just gotten a haircut and a manicure. Sporting a gold Rolex, too.

"Hey, ladies," Denise said excitedly through the cherry stem. "I think we have a stalker."

Beverly turned and searched the crowd. Her eyes landed on Ronnie. His eyes were already on her.

The smile on Ronnie's face was attractive, smooth, very come-hither.

"Yeah, I see you," Ronnie thought. What's he got, you're wondering. He looks like there's some money, Ronnie raised his glass to her. Now act like you're not interested.

Beverly turned away as if on cue then double-taked back. He was gone. She searched the crowd for him and felt a bit sad that she lost him.

Ronnie slinked through the crowd watching Beverly and imagining her thoughts, Oh, shit. I missed him. Where did he go? Damn. Bet I could have got at least a couple grand outta him. Won't make that mistake again, will you?

Ronnie loosened his tie and made his way up behind the ladies. "Hello."

Beverly whipped around.

Oh, shit! Ronnie imagined her thinking, Second chance. Quick, think of something to say.

"Hello," Beverly said. A tad squeakily.

A waitress arrived with a second round of drinks. Ronnie motioned for them to be passed to the ladies. "I like the way you ladies dance. I'm Ron Mitchell." *Now flash the bling, but not too obviously.* He used his watch hand to tip the waitress $20.

Shenique glistened like a she-wolf. Beverly didn't notice at all—she was too busy looking into his eyes.

"Thanks for the drinks, Ron," Shenique said, pointing out her entourage, "I'm Shay. That's Dee and Bev." Denise rolled her eyes at 'Shay's' pretension.

About an hour later, the four sat at a booth. Ronnie and the ladies talked over the music as they devoured plates of ribs, fish and shrimp. "So tell me," Ronnie asked, "What do you ladies do?"

"I'm a dental assistant," Shay chimed in first. "Molars, canines, root canals. We have the latest lasers, you know?"

Ronnie nodded, *$45,000. Good, but not great*, the memory of the newspaper classified ads ran through his mind. He glanced to Denise, brows raised in potential interest.

You've heard of Hammond and Gray? Denise asked, knowing that her employment wasn't the most glamorous. "The law firm? I'm the office manager."

Oooo. No bueno. Twenty-six a year. How do people live on that? He nearly wondered aloud as he looked to Beverly.

Beverly shifted a little on her chair. She didn't

like having the spotlight on her, and besides, this was beginning to feel like an interview. "I'm a photographer for the Piatro-Roget Agency."

Ding ding ding ding ding! One hundred and ten thousand plus bonuses.

"No kidding?" Ronnie said. "I almost hired you guys. Went with Leo Burnett instead. My bad. I could have met you earlier," he smiled.

"Oh?" Beverly nearly blushed. "That's sweet."

It was obvious Ron was only interested in Beverly; Shenique decided to go ahead and drop the pretense and turn the tables on Casanova. "So what about you, Ron?"

"I'm an actor," Ronnie said, taking a smidge of delight in the women's disbelief and disappointment. "Just kidding. I ran a mutual fund for some years, then retired."

"Retired?" Denise asked. "How old are you?"

"Thirty-three. I still day-trade some."

"Ron Mitchell?" Beverly suddenly remembered something, "Mitchell-Nagy Ron Mitchell? Oh, my god. I read about you years ago in *Financial Times*."

Oh, shit... She's a reader. Ronnie panicked, trying his best not to let his poker-tell show.

"You're like, some financial genius," Beverly commented. "You and Dana Nagy. She is so cool. Your partner, right? I saw her on Oprah."

"I'm sure you did," said Ronnie, trying his best not to spit.

"Oh my, Oprah Winfrey? Wait…" Shenique bobbed her head as the lyric came to mind, "'*I'm so hot, my ice dripping, baby. I got that mad luchie like*

Dana Nagy,' Dana Nagy? Really?" Shenique scooted closer to Ronnie. Hip to hip. "I love that song."

"Mmm hmm," Ronnie gritted his teeth. He hated Shenique already. "She *was* my partner," Ronnie said, scooting himself away from Shenique's hip. "We parted ways."

Shenique put on her best empathetic frowny face. "Parted ways?" She touched his thigh, "Oh, isn't that a shame."

"From what I read, you're a great role model," Beverly added.

That's right, play up the ego. You're good, girl... Perfect. He raised the Rolex to the light, checking the time, turning the watch until he saw the light it reflected beam right into each girl's eyes. "Well, ladies, it's time for me to head home. I've never been much for the party scene, honestly. Just needed to get out of the house. I'm really kind of a homebody," he said.

"Me, too," Beverly returned genuinely, but Ronnie didn't believe her. He didn't believe any woman anymore. He'd been burned and he was no longer combustible.

"You ladies have got a ride home?" Ronnie asked. "My car is right out front."

* * *

Ronnie was the perfect gentleman. He walked Beverly to her door. Beverly knew she shouldn't invite him in; however, he was kind enough to drop off Shenique and Denise and save them the cab fare, and he seemed fairly harmless. Not that she was a great judge of character in that department. Yet, the best she could be had to be better than sitting in the bottom of swimming pools and being a two-time divorcee.

"Thank you for the ride," she said at the door and felt her cheeks flush.

"You're very welcome, Beverly" Ronnie replied. Without Shenique there to irritate him, he found Beverly's genuineness quite beautiful. He was trying to keep his game going, but she was cute. Did you take those?" he asked, pointing past her to the photos lining the walls inside her apartment. "I love how they're framed."

That's all the excuse she needed; she let him inside and nodded yes. The heat in her face was rising, she knew, and just hoped it wasn't obvious.

Ronnie touched one of the black lacquer frames. "You sell these, right? Where can I buy one?"

"Oh, I don't know," Beverly said. "Too much like Ansel Adams, I think. I need to figure out my own style. Haven't found it, yet. I keep saying 'some day', but that hasn't seemed to happen yet."

"You've got a great eye. Don't sell yourself short," Ronnie said genuinely, leaning a little closer to the shot of Giordano's Pizza and reading, "Beverly Bunn-Jones-Bunn…Jones?"

"Eh, hmm," something caught in her throat as she added the latest hyphen, "—Bunn. I know, right? Beyond embarrassing."

Ronnie paused a second to take it in, then cracked up laughing. "Gave in, huh? Well, third time's a charm. I'm sure he's trying to get you back again. Beautiful lady like yourself."

Beverly dropped her eyes. The image of Mark, dripping wet and screaming, came back crystal clear. "No," she said. "Not again."

"May I call you tomorrow, Ms. Bunn?" He paused a moment and then added, "Jones-Bunn-Jones-Bunn?"

Beverly laughed, and nodded. "Yes."

Ronnie laughed, too, and kissed the back of her hand.

Beverly saw him to the door and closed it behind him. Across the room, her wedding picture still lay face down on her coffee table. She turned the dead bolt.

"Not again," she said to herself and crossed to the table. She took the picture out of the frame, and ripped it up.

Ronnie flipped on the dome light of the Mercedes and opened his AnyDo reminder calendar app on his phone. He tapped the mic button and waited for the tone to dictate his notes. *Bing.* "Had my charm set on 'Prince.' Did the Gentleman thing— no pressure. She's obviously the marrying type," he said, "Likes photography. Take her to scenic places." He paused a second and looked up at her townhouse door. His problem was that he actually like her. He thought for a second about picking someone else. Instead, he sat the phone down and shook the sappy thought of falling in love again from his mind. "Oh, yeah, Ms. Bunn Jones Bunn Jones, one hundred ten thousand dollars per year Bunn," he said to himself as he fired up Ted's Mercedes, "The hook is set. Now, just reel her in."

* * *

Modela De Carvalho struck her signature Girl From Ipanema pose for Beverly's lens. Beverly's assistant, Hector, bit his fingernails to the nubs— Modela had spent the morning wearing him out with her orders. Beverly took the camera from her eye, not liking the way Modela was framing up, and squared her fingers together.

"Hector, look..." Beverly said. "See what I mean?"

Hector peered through Beverly's fingers. Modela sneered at him.

"Angelic," said Beverly. "I want the back of her head to glow with the light. You get it now? I just need something else."

Hector climbed a ladder to adjust the lighting.

"How much longer?" Modela whined in a Portuguese accent, "God, is everyone here this slow?"

"Just a few more minutes," Beverly said through a forced grin. "Your majesty," she added with a whisper.

Modela heard the wisecrack and tilted her head slightly. "Excuse me? I usually only let Piatro take my picture. You should appreciate this opportunity, Beb-ber-bie," she said—again with the accent. Beverly wasn't sure what bothered her most about Modela—the fact that she called herself Modela, the fact that she was actually from Sandusky but pretended to be from Rio, or the fact that everyone played along with her like members of an insane cult. On more than one occasion, Beverly had been tempted to burst her bubble by asking about whether she frequented Cedar Point amusement park as a child. "Should I let Piatro know you're not ready?"

Beverly's heart missed a beat. The last thing she needed was a bad report. "No, I'm sorry, Modela. *Please*. I'm sorry. I just want to get his just right. I want to make it perfect."

"Mmm hmm. I thought so." Modela said and blew Beb-ber-bie off.

Beverly reframed the angry supermodel in her fingers. The model may have been the envy of every photographer in the nation, but there was something about the shoot that was just... missing.

A knock sounded at the door and a delivery man peeked his head inside. "Bouquet for you, Ms. Bunn," he said.

Beverly moved her fingers, framing the delivery guy instead of Modela. She framed an enormous vase of roses. Dozens of white blooms, all closed, except for one large red rose, opened and perfect in the middle.

"Those better not be from Mister Jones," Hector said, just as he reached out a little too far and knocked one of the accent lights with his elbow. It came loose and dropped towards Modela's head. Hector grabbed the cord inches from impact, but the shift in weight compromised his balance. Hector and the ladder began to fall silently, in slow motion like a cartoon, above an oblivious Modela.

Beverly was too entranced with the flowers to notice. She read the card out loud to herself, "'*There's something different about you. Please say yes to dinner with me tonight. Ronnie.'* Awww, I'm the red one?" she smiled and drank in the aroma of the flowers. She'd never seen an arrangement like it before and they were perfect. "Wait! This is it! Let's use these!" She spun around holding the vase out to Hector, just in time to see him holding his breath as he crossed the tipping point, "Watch out!" she screamed.

Modela leapt out the way just as the accent light and Hector crashed to the floor.

* * *

Shenique scraped her pick against her patient's teeth. A piece of plaque the size of a bug came off the man's second molar. "Ugh, damn," Shenique said, wiped it on his paper bib, adjusted her headset, and kept scraping. "You've only known him a week," she scolded into her mouthpiece. "And besides, them the ones you gotta watch out for."

On the other end, Beverly smelled the roses and fiddled with the petals, "He's sensitive. He's romantic…. No, he didn't. He's a gentleman. He didn't even try."

"All I know is if a man ain't trying to get no strange, he strange," Shenique said and looked her patient in the eye. "Pretend you didn't hear that."

"Mmm hmm," the patient acknowledged.

Beverly sighed. "You just don't trust men."

"Are men trustworthy?" she asked her patient.

"It depends—" Shenique jabbed the pick into

his gums.

"Noooo!" he screamed.

"See? Straight from the horse's mouth. You trust men blindly, Bev. That's why you keep giving Mark more chances."

"But Ronnie's different," Beverly said. "And he's so cute."

"Oh he's cute. I'll give you that. But," Shenique shook her head. "I don't think he's different." Shenique sat back and told her patient, "Spit."

* * *

Over the next few days, Ronnie and Beverly trekked all over Chicago taking in all the local sites.

At Millennium Park, Ronnie chased Beverly around the giant bean mirror and through the water fountains with the children.

At the art museum, Beverly drew Ronnie's face over a perfect sketch of cupid as Ronnie tried in vain to get her to add more length and girth to Cupid's endowment.

At the Willis Tower, Ronnie held Beverly over the glass box that extends four feet out from the observations deck 103 stories in the sky. Beverly pretended to scream as Ronnie put on his best sinister face for the photo they had a tourist take.

At the zoo, Ronnie made a face at a caged monkey that managed to reach his tiny hand through the bars and slap him right as Beverly clicked her camera shutter.

At Ted's house, at the end of the extended weekend, Ronnie lit candles, dimmed the lights and hid pictures of Ted, Freda and the kids. He looked good. Despite the reasons he'd initially gone after Beverly, he was falling for her and genuinely wanted to impress her.

Outside the door, Beverly matched the address in her phone's navigation to the number on the house, 1533 Champion Court. She was impressed.

The doorbell rang. Misty tried three times to jump up on the washing machine and look out the window, but she was too fat. She'd devoured half the bag of food, which she's spilled all over the floor. She took a few laps of water from the half-full roasting pan, plopped down on a giant pillow and farted. Her tail fanned the smell away.

Ronnie ushered the lovely Beverly into the home. She felt that flush return to her cheeks. Ronnie really did it for her. She didn't remember feeling this with Mark.

"Hello, there," Ronnie said, and pulled her into his arms in a hug.

She loved how his body felt in her arms. She was always a sucker for a man's hard body. "I love your home," she said.

"Thank you," Ronnie said, "I hope you love salmon, too."

She handed him a beautifully wrapped package.

Ronnie was surprised and touched, "What's this?"

"Just a little something. Open it."

He paused as he reconsidered his plan but stilled his heart against her charms. He refused to be a sucker again. He removed the bow and opened the thick foil paper. It was a wood framed picture of the monkey slapping him at the zoo. Ronnie laughed. "You really captured the monkey's rage."

"I liked the surprise on your face more."

By the end of dinner, Beverly was in love. The only thing Mark knew how to do in the kitchen was warm leftover burritos. "Delicious," Beverly said, as she wiped her mouth with the linen napkin.

"What can I say? I love to cook. Keeps me sane," Ronnie replied.

Beverly's eyes sparkled. "You're so my kinda man."

Ronnie tapped his cell phone. India Arie's *Part of My Life* echoed from the Harman/Kardon Bluetooth surround speakers. "Dance with me?" he asked, and reached for her hand.

They danced and everything was perfect in Beverly's mind. She breathed him in. He's was the one. Unless he really screwed it up, he was getting some tonight.

"May I kiss you," Ronnie said, even though he knew the answer. She knew he knew. He kissed her. Then again. Next time, she kissed him. She kissed him the next time, too, until…

Misty heard the rhythm of the bed all the way down in the laundry room. She sprawled out on her back, belly up and farted again.

* * *

Beverly nuzzled her face into the pillow. An early morning ray of sunshine cast her face in a warm glow. Her eyes blinked open, slowly. She reached to the other side of the bed and found it empty.

She sat up, wrapping the sheets around her. Beverly's mind was clouded, foggy. Where was Ronnie? Did he leave? Why would he leave his own house if he didn't want to be here when she woke up? Dear, God, was she really that bad?

"Tea?" Ronnie asked from the doorway, holding a silver tray with a service for two, and a red rose in a bud vase.

Relief washed over her. "Yes, thank you," she said, jumped up from the bed, and made a mad dash for the closet, like a naked bee.

"Hey! Where're you going?" Ronnie nearly stuttered in shock. He hadn't cleaned out his brother and sister-in-law's closet. How was he going to explain that? Freda's wardrobe? Oh, sh—

"Ron?" Beverly asked from the closet.

"Um?" he said, still perplexing.

"Whose clothes are these?"

Ronnie set the service tray on the bed and joined her in the closet.

"Those? Those are my sister-in-law's."

"Why are they in your closet?"

"I keep asking my brother the same thing," Ronnie began to explain, hoping his quick thinking would work. Although he wasn't entirely sure what he was thinking. "Messy divorce, I'm afraid. He couldn't bear to see them in his own house, so I told him he could keep them here for now, and if you see something you like, help yourself."

Beverly selected one of Ted's dress shirts and noticed a hideous forest green and brown dress. "No, I don't want anything." She rejoined Ronnie in the bedroom.

"These last two weeks have been the best of my life," Ronnie had anticipated the statement to be a gross exaggeration, but it wasn't. "You bring out a part of me I never knew existed." He seemed to lose his nerve. "Hey, how about that tea, huh?" He handed her a cup of his house blend and moved the porcelain sugar bowl to her side of the tray. "Sugar?" he asked and lifted the lid.

Beverly gasped.

Sitting inside the sugar, a diamond ring sparkled up at her.

* * *

The main phone rang at the What A Lovely Smile dental offices.

"What A Lovely Smile, how can I help you?" asked the receptionist. She pulled the phone away from her ear. Someone was shrieking on the other end. "Shenique! It's for you!"

"Hold on," Shenique called from the back. She draped a lead blanket on her patient, adjusted the X-ray cannon, and went back behind the glass. Shenique took the call from behind the glass. "This is Shenique... Girl! What's up? You okay?"

Beverly was seated on a make-up stool in the master bathroom, cupping her mouth to her cell phone, sipping on her tea.

"I can't," she said. "Hold on..." Beverly tapped the three-way icon. "You there, Denise?"

Indeed Denise was. Buried behind a pile of paper, she had to try to hide a personal call from the Hammond and Gray Law Office gestapo. "I'm here. What's the matter?"

Beverly could not contain herself. "You guys ready? He proposed!"

"I hope you said 'no'," Shenique said, zapping the X-ray cannon.

"I don't know what to say..." Beverly stammered.

"Say yes!" yelled Denise. To hell with gestapo. This was exciting! True love!

Shenique zapped her patient again. "Shut up, Denise. You say 'no', Beverly! You don't know this man! Why's he so anxious? What's the rush?"

"He says he's wasted enough time. He wants a wife and family," Beverly said, and ran her fingers across a 600 thread count bath towel. "And you gotta see his house," she whispered.

But Beverly's whisper was quite audible to anyone standing outside the master bathroom door. Ronnie sneered, victorious—he knew it—she was just like the others. He reeled in an invisible fish with and invisible rod and walked back over to the bed.

Beverly sighed happily. "Of course, I don't care about the house. He just wants my love."

"Wow," Denise said, impressed. "He sounds just like you."

Beverly smiled.

Shenique, however, was not. "You hush, Denise!"

"No, you hush, Shenique!" Denise was sick and tired of Shenique's bitter-bitch behavior. "We've been subscribing to your romance advice since high school, and none of us are happy. So I'm canceling my subscription. Beverly?

"Yes," Beverly said, quietly. She'd never heard Denise go in on Shenique before.

"Just DO it," Denise went on. "Who knows how many chances'll come your way? You know… I mean… uh,… with someone other than Mark."

Shenique seethed. "I'm gonna come over to that office and dot your eye in a minute," she warned.

"You go right ahead," Denise returned.

Click.

Beverly checked her phone. She had only one caller now. "Hello?"

"Beverly, this is your chance. Grab it. The best you can be!"

Denise disconnected herself from the call.

Beverly glanced down at the neatly-arranged magazine holder. An Oprah magazine sat front and center. The cover story was entitled, *Follow Your Heart to Love*. Beverly grinned. Ronnie read Oprah, too.

That was all the confirmation she needed.

Beverly wrapped Ted's dress shirt around her a little tighter, like a hug, and finished the rest of her tea. Man, was she hungry.

* * *

Later that afternoon, Beverly was still hungry. She couldn't understand why she had such a veracious appetite. And felt so wobbly. It must be love.

"Dare," Beverly giggled. She'd never played Strip Truth or Dare before. She was losing, but didn't mind. She brushed her bra away from her ear and took another sip of tea.

"Okay..." Ronnie said and adjusted his boxer briefs against his head. "I dare you to go to Gary, Indiana."

Beverly laughed, hard. "No way! For what?"

"Gary's a fun little city," Ronnie said.

"Gary ain't no city," Beverly chortled. "It's a suburb… of Hell."

"They got casinos. They got a bus'll pick you up and take you there. I dare you to take the bus to Gary."

* * *

An ad for Trump Riverboat Casino featured the Donald himself, holding handfuls of cash. Emblazoned above him, the words *Come get my money… y'all!"* The image rolled down the highway, as the bus belched diesel fumes behind it.

The bus wasn't particularly crowded — a few old folk looking to make their fortunes on the slot machines, okie white teens, and an old man with a loose tooth. He kept flicking it with his tongue, watching his reflection in the glass.

Ronnie and Beverly sat in the back, a thermos of Jamaican Green tea between them.

"So what do you want to do in Gary?" Beverly asked.

Ronnie glanced out the window, and saw a road-sign for Mike's Trout Farm—Big Catches Guaranteed!

"Same thing they do in Vegas," said Ronnie and poured Beverly another cup.

Chapter Four

Beverly awoke from the world's strangest dream. There was a midget in a tuxedo, playing *Here Comes the Bride* on an accordion in a small, smokey chapel. The priest was an old man with a bad orange toupee, and she'd held a bouquet of fuzzy white-rose buds, which she had to give back at the end of the ceremony.

She rubbed her eyes and felt something strange on her hand — on her finger, more specifically, the ring finger of her left hand, even more specifically. She sat up, glanced over to Ronnie, and saw the same thing on the ring finger of his left hand.

"Ronnie!" Beverly screamed.

Ronnie bolted up, as if someone stabbed him with a cattle prod. "Whaaa….. Screaming like that?"

"What did we do?" she asked, showing him her ring, grabbing his hand and showing him his.

"We got married, baby," Ronnie yawned and stretched his naked, muscular body.

Beverly stared at the muscles tightening and loosening all around him. He had Mark beat for sure. She could not help but smile. Beverly then stared at the diamond on her hand. There was still some sugar in the setting.

"Tell you what," began Ronnie. "We get a cab, and I'll drop you off at the apartment. Then I'll go pick up some of my things and meet you over there."

Confusion whirled in Beverly's mind like a dervish. She couldn't wrap her head around what had happened. What was happening?

"What? Why would you come to the apartment?"

Ronnie propped himself up on his elbow. "You'll mess up your credit if you break your lease. Besides, you don't want to move into a house you didn't pick out, do you?"

"But… I like your house," Beverly said, still glued to the ring.

"Wait a minute… You didn't marry me for the house, did you?"

Beverly shook her head. This was all happening so fast. She couldn't believe it was happening at all. "No, no, of course not. I'm just –"

"Good. You had me worried for a minute," Ronnie said, then got out of bed, kissed his bride and slow-jogged to the bathroom.

She watched his ass as he did and shook her head. *Mmm, that's all mine*, she thought. Beverly put her hands to her face, then drew them down. The ring felt weird on her finger. "Sucker for love," she said.

* * *

Upon his triumphant return to Chicago, the first thing Ronnie saw to was depositing six thousand dollars back into Ted's account. The second thing he saw to was the quality of the paint job provided by

Jose's Handy Hombre Services. He'd given Jose a thousand in cash, plus a hundred dollar tip.

Ronnie stood on the front porch of his brother's house, his duffel bag slung over his shoulder, and almost three thousand bucks in his pocket.

He patted his pocket and started down the walkway before it hit him. "The CAT!" He ran back to the house and made his way to the laundry room. The odor assaulted him as soon as he opened the door. "Damn!" he screamed and held his breath as he opened the window and slammed the door shut again. He searched the house until he found a fan and returned to the scene of the crime. "Cats! Ugh." He plugged in the fan and turned it on high to clear out the funk.

In the room, Misty had devoured the entire twenty-pound bag of food and filled up her litterbox. She lay sprawled out on her kitty couch like a fat diva. "What the hell, cat? You ate the whole bag, you greedy bastard!" Misty belched her disinterest and licked her butt. "And you stink." Ronnie turned on the water in the utility sink and tested it for warmth. He added shampoo and grabbed the cat. Misty screeched, but was too out of shape to put up her normal fight. She plopped into the water and resigned her fate.

Ronnie scrubbed the cat vigorously and then sat her on the top of the washing machine. "Stay," he commanded and ran out the room in search of a hair dryer. He checked all four bathrooms to no avail. He dried Misty with a towel and noticed a shoe dryer rack. He picked it up and thought about it. The cat seemed to say no, but Ronnie was desperate. He put the rack in the dryer and thought about the wisdom of the action he contemplated. "Just a few minutes okay? You can sit still for a few minutes can't you?" He studied the cat's face for a second. "Of course you can. You sat here while I went upstairs. Where are you going to go? You're too fat," he was convincing himself now. He sat Misty on the dryer rack and closed the door. He set the dryer to no heat. He thought about it again and opened the door to check. Misty had not moved. In fact, she was lying down again, unconcerned. Ronnie shut the door again and started the dryer. He looked through the door to check—she seemed unconcerned. "She'll be fine," Ronnie said to himself and started cleaning up the rest of the room.

He dumped the litter in a garbage bag and refilled the box. He grabbed the cat bed and threw it in the washing machine. He mopped the floor and then tossed the food bag in with the litter and took it outside to the trashcans.

When he returned, he heard a thumping sound. "YOU MOVED?! NO! NO!" He raced to the dryer and ripped the door open. Misty's hair stood on end the size of a beach ball. Ronnie spent a minute trying to figure out which way to grab the cat. He pulled out the ball of fur and sat it down. He tried to find the legs, the head, the tail. It all ran together. As he prodded blindly, Misty screeched, and Ronnie yanked his hand back, "Sorry girl," he said, then turned her over to her feet and sat her on the floor. The ball of fur walked along the floor and out the room. Ronnie exhaled his relief.

"Wow, great job, Ronnie," Ted said as he looked over the paint job. The house looked brand new.

"I have to admit, I didn't expect it to come out this good," even his archenemy, Freda, could not hold back the smile. "Okay, come on," she stretched out her arms in a hug for Ronnie. Ronnie reluctantly moved into her embrace.

"MOM!!! Something wrong with Misty!"

Freda turned cold instantly. She knew it. "What'd you do?!"

The ball waddled into the room followed by the two boys staring in terror. "RONNIE!" Ted yelled.

"You said feed her. You didn't say how much."

"You could have called us!"

"I didn't want to disturb you."

Freda went to her cat's aid, "Oh baby," she cooed as she reached down to pick the cat up. Static electricity released from the cat and transferred to Freda instead. The electric pop shocked Freda, but Misty's hair returned to normal. "Oh, there you are." Misty purred. "You're okay. You put on a little weight, uh?" She struggled holding the fat cat. "Uncle Ronnie is an idiot, I know."

The room fell quiet except for the snickers of the two boys.

Ted and Ronnie stared uncomfortably just above Freda's eye level.

"What?!" She demanded.

Rather than answer, Ted showed Ronnie to the door. Ronnie said his goodbyes and slunk away quickly.

"At least he didn't kill her," Freda said and carried her cat out of the room.

Ted watched his wife retreat, her hair standing on end from the static electricity that had transferred to her. He wondered how long it would take her to notice.

"RONNIE YOU ASSHOLE!" Freda screamed as she passed the powder room and caught a glimpse of herself in the mirror! "TED!"

Ted quickly ran up the stairs.

"IMMATURE PRICK!"

* * *

Elliott Bunn's eyes narrowed to slits as he chewed his collard greens. He did not trust, like, or care for fancy-pants Ronnie Mitchell, sitting at his table and breaking bread with him. A man was to ask a father's permission to court, let alone marry, his daughter. Elliott's wife, and subsequently Beverly's mother, Wanda, felt the same way. Although in Wanda's estimation, Ronnie was quite a catch. She'd just wished Beverly had introduced him before they got married. Such is the impetuousness of youth.

Ronnie choked down another forkful of collard greens. God, he hated that stuff. "I finished Yale, top ten percentile of my class," he said. "Started a real estate firm in –"

"Mmmwhayou do now, mmm? Elliott asked in his thick southern drawl that no one born outside of Mississippi could possibly understand.

"Daddy, he's getting to that," Beverly explained.

Elliott took hold of the butter knife. "Mmmthe man emgimme straight answer!"

Wanda patted Elliot's hand. The one with the knife. "No one's good enough for your baby," she said soothingly. "You did this same thing to poor Mark. Be happy anybody else married her."

"Mmmtellmewhat you do?" Elliott asked, without it sounding too much like a question. Or, anything.

"Excuse me?" said Ronnie.

"He's an entrepreneur," Beverly put on her best smile.

"Mmmapimp."

Beverly gasped. "Daddy! An investor. He invests money in businesses."

Elliot's butter knife scraped the dish as he stared bullets at Ronnie. "Mmmellme work for?"

"I beg your pardon?" Ronnie said, his brows in a perpetual state of knit.

"He works for himself, Daddy."

Elliott tossed the butter knife to the table. He'd heard enough. He got up from the table and headed to the living room. The sounds of *Sports Center* emanated from within. Wanda placed her napkin on her plate and left the room.

Beverly turned to Ronnie, a slight blush of embarrassment on her cheeks.

"Mmmmanaintgot no job. Mmmhima playboy," Elliott's voice admonished from the other room.

"I'm so sorry," Beverly said.

"Do you think that's bad?" asked Ronnie.

* * *

Normally, Mrs. Mitchell would have been delighted to have her whole family gathered around the table. Just like the good old days. This evening was their first without Ronald Senior, and that was hard enough. However, there was a new face here tonight. A face that hadn't been introduced nor spoken of until now, so learning that this face was now a part of the Mitchell family tree... well... it wasn't going so well. Doubly difficult to tell, too, since no one had said a word all night.

Freda dragged her fork through her untouched mashed potatoes and noticed a button missing on the sleeve of her favorite green dress. Then, she returned her relentless, unyielding stare at Beverly Bunn-Jones-Bunn-Jones-Bunn-Mitchell. Good Lord in the highest heaven, how STUPID was her brother in law, anyway?

Linda and Jeff busied themselves with an occasional glance at each other. Mrs. Mitchell glanced at them, glancing at each other. Beverly, the poor dear, appeared as though she was the lamb at a sacrificial dinner, which, in essence, she was. Mrs. Mitchell folded her hands beneath her chin, her eyes sparkling at Ronnie. She could forgive him for eloping. Heck, she and Ronald Senior had done the same thing. And his wife did seem like a nice girl. Mrs. Mitchell just wished she would speak. It would have been easier to figure her out, that way.

Ronnie, never at a loss for words, sat in absolute silence.

The only sound was chewing.

Then choking, as a spoonful of succotash lodged in Jeff's throat. He tried to gasp for breath, but no breath could get passed the lima bean.

All eyes turned to him, more irritated than concerned. Jeff was always choking, even on water.

Beverly jabbed Ronnie on the shoulder as if to say "shouldn't somebody do something?", but her concern would prove to be unfounded. Jeff slugged himself in the sternum and spat out the lima bean onto Freda. It matched her dress.

* * *

Beverly came into her apartment loaded down with canvas bags from the grocery store. She'd picked up some candy canes and eggnog for the approaching holidays and about a thousand other things – exotic things like milk, eggs, butter, and bread, because apparently Ronnie couldn't be bothered. Beverly could see why. He was unbelievably busy, obviously, watching the Bears lose to the green Bay Packers — by a lot. Ronnie was entertaining company, too, a wiry looking guy whom Beverly had never before seen.

"Damn!" the stranger announced. Final score, Bears 3, Packers 24. "That's five g's you owe Butter."

"*I* owe him?" Ronnie accused. "What about you?"

Beverly began unpacking the bags. She slammed down a can of green beans.

"Oh, hey, babe," Ronnie acknowledged without turning around. "This is Moe."

"Nice to meet you... Moe," Beverly waited for Moe to return the sentiment.

Moe chugged Ronnie on the head. "Ron Ron, I don't bet the games anymore. Not since you hipped me up on that day tradin' and I got that pastoring gig at ya momma's church," he said, then leaned closer. "Just a word of advice, yo. It's due at five PM tomorrow. Don't be late."

Another can of vegetables pounded against the granite counter tops. Beverly's passive-aggressive grab for attention wasn't working. Irritated, she looked down at the mail. Well, at least her husband took time from his busy schedule to bring that into the apartment. Only one of the envelopes that was not a bill, but a rather happy looking envelope – an invitation of some sort that at on top of the pile. The names of the senders was familiar. Ted and Freda Mitchell. However, so was the address, 1533 Champion Court. Ronnie's house.

Beverly picked up the envelope, checking and double checking the address. Which, after the third double check, was as confusing as ever. She placed it on top of another mailer – her Oprah Winfrey magazine. The top article — "Is Your Man Who You Think He Is?"

Moe chugged down the last drop in his thermos and belched. "If you want that money back, sell Teledosis Systems short. Word is they got sunk on their sonic toothbrush division. They're going chapter thirteen."

"You know I don't mess with the market anymore," Ronnie said, more to his cup of tea than Moe.

"Your loss," Moe said as he got up from the sofa. "I gotta go teach Bible study." He grabbed his thermos and began making his way past the kitchen.

"Nice to meet you, Beverly. Have a nice day at work?"

"Fabulous."

"Great. Hey, I really like your pictures. You should sell those."

Beverly's expression remained unchanged. "Thanks."

Moe showed himself to the door. "Five PM, yo," he reminded Ronnie. "Butter plays for keeps," he said right before he left.

"So, babe," Beverly began. The invitation sat on Oprah's smiling face. "I was wondering... what did you do with all the furniture from the house?"

Five g's. Five g's to big ol' Butter, Ronnie thought, then remembered he'd just been asked a question — a good question. One he knew he'd have to answer, eventually, but *five g's?* "Oh, that? I, um, I sold it to Ted and Freda. When they bought the house and the car."

"You must have gotten some good money for all that," Beverly stated.

"Barely broke even."

Beverly didn't like the tone of his voice. He sounded as if he was making this up as he went along. "Speaking of a house, the lease is up this month. And we haven't even started –"

Beverly looked up, to find Ronnie had left the room.

A moment later, the toilet flushed.

Ronnie sat on the john, pants still down, reading his checkbook register. He rubbed his face. Each entry was a steady decrease of balance. Each entry, a cash withdraw. Each week, a thousand dollars less. Ronnie studied the transactions, dating all the way back to his appropriated funds for Ted's home improvement project. The next entry read *Xfer from Beverly* then, the balance back to zero. Two more entries, both attributed to Xfer from Beverly and again, the standard zero.

A grin etched on Ronnie's face. He entered, $2,000 Xfer from Beverly.

"Dude, you should have thought of this shit earlier," he said, so proud of himself he could bust. "This is the life. Maybe women are just smarter than men."

Ronnie reached behind him and flushed the toilet once more.

* * *

It was unusually warm this Christmas season. The sidewalks of Michigan Avenue, normally piled with snow, were just slick with wet run-off and melting sleet. Beverly, Shenique, and Denise made their way down the Magnificent Mile, arms hooked together like a big paper chain trying to keep their balance.

Beverly distracted herself with her old standby – window shopping. It doesn't cost you anything to look. And that red leather jacket in the window was definitely worth looking at. Too bad she couldn't afford to take it off the mannequin.

"All of it?" Denise asked, disbelieving. "The whole Christmas fund?"

"I told you. Didn't I tell you?" Shenique

clenched her arm around Beverly's a little tighter, mostly to keep from falling on the slick sidewalk, but also because she was pissed off. "But noooo. Listen to old desperate Denise. He was playing you from jump street."

"And you know what?" Beverly began, hardly wanting to admit what she was about to, "I don't think he ever owned that house. I think it's been his brother's all along."

"He's still your husband," chimed Denise, in her silver-lining-in-every-cloud kind of way. "And he has a degree from Yale. He's smart."

Shenique unhooked her arm from Denise. "Please! George Bush had a degree from Yale," she pointed an accusatory finger at Beverly. "He's smart enough to trick her lonely ass into marrying him, though. The man's got issues. Deep issues. Need to call some brothers from back in Jersey to kick his ass. Issues."

"Just talk to him, Bev. Be direct. And firm. Tell him you expect more from a Yale man."

Shenique drew her fist back, ready to pop their resident Pollyanna. Denise cowered behind Beverly.

"Kick his ass to the curb!" Shenique screamed.

A few passers-by gave the angry woman and her friends a wide, wide berth as they made their way around them.

* * *

The click, click, clack of a computer keyboard echoed throughout the bedroom. Ronnie was at the computer, a few beads of sweat dotted against his brow. He squinted at the screen that read;

Short Teledosis – 500 shares for $2

Ronnie wiped his face, and shook his head to clear it. He moved the arrow to Place Order.

Current Price/Share $4

"I hope it drops soon," he said to himself. He would talk to himself a lot, particularly when playing the market at night. There were other things he'd rather be doing at night, for sure, and she just came into the bedroom.

Beverly buttoned the top of her flannel nightgown and drew the covers down.

"Something wrong?"

"Yeah," she returned and crawled into bed. She promptly pulled the blanket over her head.

A look of fairly uncharacteristic concern drew across Ronnie's face. "Something I did?

Nothing from Beverly. Only a quiet weeping.

"Hey..." Ronnie said and went to her side. "Wait a minute… babe..."

"Ronnie, do you love me?"

"I've never loved anybody more," he said, not missing a beat.

"Then why are you using me?" asked Beverly, her voice muffled underneath the blanket.

Caught. Red-handed. Well, he knew it was coming. But for some strange reason, he felt a sour little tinge in his gut like a conscious.

Beverly turned toward him but kept her face hidden in the sheet. "I keep telling myself that, if I just don't say anything and wait, you'll figure it out. You'll become the man I know you can be. That you'll stop taking advantage of me." She pulled the covers from her face. It was wet with tears.

"Wait one damn minute," Ronnie said. His little conscious-tinge suddenly replaced by anger. "Why's it okay that millions of women stay home every day spending their husband's money, and it's not 'taking advantage'"?

"Raising children," Beverly defended.

"No. Not all of 'em. They're watching soap operas, and Oprah, and going to the spa. I know. I see them every day. But when I do it, I'm using you? You got some nerve," Ronnie said. "You act like you're poor and struggling. This ain't the 1950's— you make more money than most men. You ain't hurting. You ain't suffering. I ain't putting you through shit. You know what I've been through in my life? The pain? The grief? All my shit got took! I thought you cared. You don't care about me."

Beverly sat up, unbelieving. "Care about you? You're the man. You're supposed –"

"Supposed to what? Work like a dog so my woman can spend my money? Well, no thank you. I already played the fool, and I didn't like it."

"Neither do I, asshole!"

Ronnie got up from the bed, and began to pace. He massaged his forehead trying to calm himself down but it wasn't working. "You knew I wasn't working when we got together. I didn't lie to you. You *thought* I had money. That's on you! You should have asked. But, see, you married me to get your hands on me lucky charms, and now, you're pissed off 'cause I ain't got shit no more. Boo hoo."

Beverly snatched the covers back over her head, and turned her back to him.

"Ronnie, I'm not Dana."

Ronnie wasn't interested. He headed to the door. "You're full of shit, though. Just like her and every other woman," he said as he left and slammed the door behind him.

In a semi-pathetic act of wrath – but mostly frustration – Beverly had taken a book from the nightstand and hurled it at Ronnie but hit the closed door instead.

Ronnie stuck his head back inside the door, "You missed!" He stuck out his tongue. Beverly hurled another, but Ronnie was too quick. The second book hit the back of the door. "MISSED AGAIN!" Ronnie yelled from the hallway.

* * *

There were only a few shopping weeks until Christmas, and the store room at Bloomingdale's was stocked for the rush. The store manager, looking at the heaps of boxes of display items ready for presentation, flipped on his little television. The screen warmed up to the current broadcast – *The Oprah Winfrey Show.*

The main floor looked as if the holidays threw up on it. Oversized presents, blinking lights against a forest of fake trees, and an animatronic Santa waving from a Styrofoam sign that proclaimed this was the North Pole. Right next to Santa, an empty table waited to be filled with *Oprah's Favorite Things!*

It wasn't just Bloomingdale's ready for the latest retail onslaught. Wal-Mart was right on board with holiday excess, as well. Wrapping paper, bows, chocolate Santas, and electronic razor kits all in a row decked these particular halls.

A large woman in a small dress came through the doors, checking her coupon circular. Wal-Mart Greeter Saul welcomed her with a big kiss and a quick pat of her ass. "Welcome to Wal-Mart," Saul chirped happily. "Here's a cart!" he said and wheeled one of the trollies toward her.

The woman situated her coupons in front of her for easy access and passed by a store television airing Oprah's show.

"It's that time of year!" Oprah sang. "We're doing My Favorite Things. I love this stuff!"

As Oprah's signature theme music began, an orchestrated jazz fusion with a funky snare drum rhythm, shoppers gathered around the set.

At the New York Stock Exchange, people did the same. Brokers, runners, and every pit hung on the next words to be uttered from the TVs. The jazz fusion with a chirpy snare drum faded. Oprah held up her first Favorite Thing for the camera, a Sonic Motion toothbrush.

"This toothbrush is fabulous," Oprah proclaimed.

And oh yay, oh yay, the world responded.

The Bloomingdale's manager grabbed the mic from the store P.A. "Sonic Motion Toothbrushes!"

Stock boys ran like ants on fire, snatching every box of Sonic Motion Toothbrushes in the room.

The effect was felt at Bartlesby Fund, as well. Bill and Harry – the boys in matching blue suits – flew into Dana Nagy's corner office. One of her personal flat screens was tuned to the Oprah Show.

"Who makes those damn toothbrushes?" Dana shouted. Time was money, people.

Bill queried an app on his phone, "Teledosis Systems."

Dana stood up from her desk, and pounded it. "Buy Teledosis! Buy it now!" ordered Dana. She fixed her attention to her computer, where Teledosis Systems stock was climbing from four dollars to six.

"I love how it makes my mouth tingle," Oprah said through a grin. "Isn't it great?"

"Buy! Buy! Buy!" a broker on the NYSE floor screamed, and he wasn't the only one.

The board displayed the Teledosis stock for the world to see. Eight dollars to ten. Then fourteen.

Wal-Mart shoppers, looking like an apocalyptic version of their popular internet site, showed no mercy as they clamored for the coveted Toothbrush. Carts slammed into each other, clothes were torn, and hair was pulled, until the Sonic Toothbrush section was emptied.

Saul the greeter smiled at the television, Oprah's face shining down on him. It was almost holy.

"Socket Motion toothbrushes. I'll be. In my day, a little bakin' soda on yer finger'd do ya fine," he said and picked at his one remaining tooth.

At precisely ten o'clock, the doors to

Bloomingdale's opened. Ninety percent of the city's population squished their way through, pouring to the sacred isle of *Oprah's Favorite Things!* They attacked it like a river of piranha.

Seconds later, it was empty.

The only person on the planet unaware of the season's Hottest Item was Ronnie. He had been in the shower, trying to wash off the disgust of last night and failing miserably. He walked through the empty bedroom and sat at the computer. He rubbed his eyes and waited for his investment web site to come up. Ronnie moved the cursor to Teledosis. And clicked.

Teledosis - $35/share.

Ronnie's jaw dropped to his knee caps. He began typing furiously.

Updating…

"C'mon, c'mon..." he said. His screen couldn't possibly be right.

Teledosis - $45/share.

Ronnie slumped back in the chair. Then slumped further as…

REMINDER: Total due on trade: $20,000.

"Oh, my God," Ronnie whispered and flashed on those images of people jumping out of windows when the market crashed in '29. "Why did I listen to Moe?"

This is the life, Ron Ron.

Chapter Five

S henique was having a hell of a time trying to clean her latest patient's teeth. The woman kept crying, having to take several breaks to wipe the snot away from her nose. On the lighter side, the Sonic Motion toothbrush was a dream to use. What A Lovely Smile kept a stockpile of them in storage for the past few years. After Oprah's holiday proclamation, however, the office had to keep them under lock and key.

"Rinse," Shenique said.

Beverly spat into the little sink. And sniffled.

Shenique sighed and used the overhead monitor to query an old episode of Oprah on YouTube. "Here, girl. Look at this. I went through some of these for you... maybe now you'll listen."

An episode of the Oprah Winfrey Show began playing on the exam room's flat screen. Shenique crossed her arms and kept a very close eye on Beverly, hoping for the light to come on in her Novocained head.

On the screen, Oprah adjusted her flowing skirt against her lap. Her face became serious. "It's 'Valuing Yourself', with Gary Zukav. Have you ever felt undervalued?"

A member of Oprah's audience raised her hand. The stage runner placed a microphone for her.

"My husband takes me for granted," she said. "I try so hard to please him..."

Gary Zukav, the fifty something regular guest of Oprah, leaned forward with sincerity and firmness. Very firm. Gary was a former monk turned psychologist, and one of the most popular psyche experts in the country. His advice was golden, as Gary was the first to confirm.

"You have to value *yourself*," Gary explained.

"So true, Gary," agreed Oprah. "If I had a husband who didn't appreciate me, I would leave him. Wouldn't even think twice about it. Life's too short. Leave now. Gary..?"

Gary nodded. "I agree wholeheartedly. Because, as you all know, I used to be a monk. Had I held on to my monkness, I would never have been on TV. There are many monks. But not many on TV. I took a risk," he said and took a thoughtful pause. "What I'm saying is, don't monk around with your life."

"Life is hard enough," Oprah said, accentuating Gary's comment. She took a long, hard look at the audience member with the ungrateful husband. "You need to leave and get yourself together."

Applause rose from the studio.

Shenique turned off the television, picked up a small mirror, and held it to Beverly's face.

"And, your lease is up now, too?" she asked, without being subtle.

Beverly took the mirror and studied her reflection. She saw herself very, very clearly. As scary as it was, she knew what she had to do. Starting the journey to being the best one could be was always scary.

Ronnie shifted nervously as he stood in front of the Citibank teller. His signature at the bottom of the transfer slip looked as if it was signed by someone with epilepsy. He'd come across smooth, though — calm, relaxed, no worries.

"I'm sorry, sir" the teller said, not sounding sorry at all. "But this account was just closed."

"What?" Ronnie said too loudly. A flare of nerves surged through his stomach. Butterflies with nails for wings. He cleared his throat. "Just advance it against this." He passed the teller a Visa card, embossed with Beverly's name.

The teller ran the card through the reader, then handed it back to Ronnie. "This one's closed, too."

"Closed? What the hell?" A brand new sort of ire coursed through Ronnie's veins. Beverly had betrayed him. Slyly. "She's smart," he seethed beneath his breath.

"Thank you," the teller said with a smile.

"Not you," Ronnie retorted and stormed out of the bank.

Later that night, Ronnie sat on the edge of the bed, wringing his hands. His voice was trembling and soft.

"Bev, baby… I know I've done wrong. I'm in the hole for twenty grand…" he sniffed. "I'm getting a job, though. I'll work something out… but there's this guy I borrowed from. His name's… his name…" Another sniff and a snort. "His name's Butter and if I don't pay him, I'm dead. And I know I've blown

through a lot of money. But, never again, I swear,"
Ronnie drew in a huge breath. "I love you, Bev.
Give me another chance. Please, baby. Please. I –"

Ronnie's phone rang. He sighed, disgusted,
and tapped Accept. It was Beverly calling.

"Hello?... oh, really? What happened...?
Yeah, I'll come get you," he said and disconnected the
call. "Oh sure. Now she needs me. 'Oh, help me,
Ronnie! My car broke down!'"

Ronnie walked across the room to the closet.
Maybe this would work out better than he had though.
He gets to be the hero. How do you refuse a hero?

Two figures lay in hiding just outside the
apartment. Beverly bit down on her lip and crouched
a little further in the bushes. Shenique pulled a twig
out of her hair and froze. Ronnie had come out of the
main doors. He crossed the street, got in his car, and
drove away.

"It's go time," Shenique said, putting her
fingers in her mouth then whistling.

A U-Haul truck pulled up to the curb.

An El train rumbled across the tracks.
Ronnie's car was underneath, rolling along past
Austin Avenue in Oak Park, at least an hour's drive
from where he and Beverly lived and where Beverly
claimed she was broken down. Ronnie challenged
himself to turn on his tears again. Now, not only was
he about to become the knight in shining armor but a
humble knight as well.

"I know it's hard to trust me, babe, but I had
an epiphany. I really love you," he snuffled. "You're

right. I used you. I don't know why. But I'm going to get some counseling and figure it out."

Ronnie parked his car at the intersection, expecting to see Beverly's Accord, hood up and helpless. All he saw, however, was a dog taking a piss on a hydrant.

He pulled out his phone and dialed Beverly's cell. It went straight to voicemail. Curious. Maybe her battery is dead. *Poor baby*, he thought, *at least she's in a decent neighborhood*. He dialed their home number; he couldn't think of anything else to do. He leaned back and waited for the landline to answer. Beverly's voice came through loud and clear.

"Hi, you've reached casa de Mitchell," she announced. Ronnie's brow creased. That wasn't their message. "If this is Ronnie, I want you to know I'm alright. I got a ride. I'll explain when you get here. Leave a message if you want!"

Beep.

"You're at the house, and you didn't call me, but you took the time to change the voicemail? Really? Are you serious, right now?" Ronnie waited for her to pick up. She didn't. "Beverly!" He waited again. "Bev!" Still nothing. He bit his lip. Something wasn't right. Ronnie disconnected the call, threw the car in drive, and sped off.

There wasn't a light on in the apartment. Ronnie fumbled for the light switch. "Bev? Beverly, what happened? I was worried about you. I didn't know what —" Ronnie's voice cut off as the lights came on. The apartment was completely abandoned.

"Beverly?? Where's all our stuff?" He said before he stopped to think.

Ronnie ran to the living room where only one item remained — the flat screen.

A DVD was next to the television. Upon it, a Post-It note instructed: "Play Me."

Ronnie looked left, right, then left again. Panic set in.

The DVD player was gone, too.

* * *

Ted was attempting to open a new package of bright blue plastic ornaments from Target – the way they packaged these things you'd think they were made out of plutonium – when his doorbell rang and rang and rang and rang. Misty sat at the door, her tail twitching. Ted stepped over her as he answered the door.

"Butter kidnapped Beverly!" Ronnie shouted and ran inside, almost tripping over the cat.

"Who?" Ted asked. "What?"

Ronnie rushed to the entertainment center and powered up the DVD player. "He left this and took everything in the house."

"What?" Ted asked again, watching his brother pry the disc from its case and put it in the player.

Freda came in from the kitchen, wiping sugar-cookie dough from her fingers. "Ted, who was at the –" she saw Ronnie plugging in a DVD. Her expression went cold. "Oh."

"Ron says somebody kidnapped Beverly," Ted explained.

Ronnie pushed *play* and sat back nervously.

Oprah's face filled the screen. "Have you ever felt undervalued?" she asked.

Forty two minutes later (commercials had been edited) Ronnie and Ted were statue still. Freda looked a little smug sitting on the recliner; Misty curled up on her lap.

"Looks to me like somebody wised up and got sick of your shit," she said, pointing at the television. "It reminds me, Ted, that they're all out of those Sonic Motion toothbrushes Oprah was talking about today. May have to special order for your grandma."

"Those what?" Ronnie queried.

"Electric toothbrushes. Oprah likes them."

Ted nodded. "Yeah, that Teledosis stock went through the roof. That's the kind of deal you used to get in on, remember?"

Ronnie gritted his teeth and began to pace. Oprah, again? The goddess of daytime bullshit? The one who somehow kept ruining his life?

"At least nobody kidnapped Beverly," Freda said and got up from her recliner, dislodging Misty. The cat growled and slunk off underneath the coffee table. "You're a bum, Ronnie. I saw the money you took out of our account. You're lucky I don't sue you."

"I'm not a bum, Freda," Ronnie defended, catching a quick glimpse of Misty staring at him with her hateful cat eyes.

"Yeah, you are," said Ted. He'd seen the missing money, too.

Ronnie took a moment, contemplating his next move. He didn't know how they knew about the missing funds – which he'd replaced. He guessed he could have been a little more sly about the transactions, but he was preoccupied. In the meantime, there was a gangster breathing down his neck.

"Look, guys..." Ronnie began. "This is probably a bad time, but I need five grand. If I don't pay Butter, I'm dead."

Ted shook his head. "Ronnie, you're foul, bro. I don't even know you anymore. You get yourself into shit I can't even imagine. I can't help you."

"You need to leave," Freda said in no uncertain terms.

Ted ejected the DVD, handed it to his little brother, and saw him to the door. There were no words exchanged between them. For some moments in life, there are none. But there was for this one, "I shouldn't have bought this house for y'all," Ronnie said at the door. "You ungrateful bastards."

"Get help, Ronnie." Freda yelled from safe inside the living room.

"You get help; you frigid bitch."

Freda froze in place. Ted's eyes ignited with betrayal. The one secret Ronnie was never supposed to reveal.

"Goodnight, big bro," Ronnie added with a sarcastic and evil smirk, knowing full-well Ted would not have a good night for many, many weeks, if ever again.

Ronnie closed the door behind him and something smashed into it. Misty screeched. "YOU SON OF A BITCH!" Ronnie heard Freda scream before he got out of earshot down the driveway. Ted was getting his just deserts. Ted will be lucky if he escapes uninjured.

Ronnie's keys turned in the lock. Not that locking the apartment was necessary, there was nothing left to take except the telephone which was blinking with messages. A dash of hope ran through him. He pushed *play* expecting to hear Beverly begging for forgiveness or at least offering a reasonable explanation.

Instead of Beverly's voice, he heard his own, asking Beverly to pick up if she was there.

Ronnie pressed three to delete the message. *BEEP.*

The next message was a man's throaty, important sounding voice. A smooth, Bostonian accent said; "This is Steve Arpin of Charles Schwab. As you know, all trades must be funded by the end of the day. Our records show that your account is off twenty thousand dollars for a bearish position on Teledosis Systems. You must fund this account in twenty four hours to avoid legal action."

Ronnie pressed three and deleted that one as well. *BEEP.* The fun was just beginning.

"This is Butter," a man said in a deep baritone. "I know yo ass ain't playin' me. Holla."

BEEP.

Butter's voice came on again. "Where you at, fool?"

BEEP.

"You bet not be home! I'll be there in ten minutes," Butter threatened then spoke to someone else in the room. "Get my gat! Boy ain't got no—" *BEEP.*

Ronnie pressed nine. A computer voice read

the timestamp, "Message left at 9:10pm." Ronnie checked his cell phone. It read 9:20. *Oh, shit*.

BOOM, BOOM, BOOM!, like a battering ram, sounded against the front door.

"Open up!" Butter yelled from the hallway.

Ronnie made a mad dash out the kitchen door. Thank God Beverly had a downstairs apartment.

The front door burst open. Butter, all six-foot eight, 310 pound, offensive linebacker of him, filled the door frame perfectly. His boys were all under five-foot-six. Butter liked it that way.

"All his shit is gone," Butter said, scanning the apartment.

One of his boys, just shy of five-foot-two, asked; "Over five grand? That stud musta hit rock bottom."

Butter nodded his substantial head. He had one of those necks that was layered with tiers of muscle. "And, he's runnin' like a punk."

A heavy rain pounded against the roof. Shenique rather liked the sound. Her mom always said raindrops were angel tears, and Shenique appreciated the fact angels must be big and badass to make noise like that. She squirted the last of the Reddi-Whip on top of two bowls of Cherry Garcia. She and Beverly were in the middle of an Oprah Winfrey Show marathon binge, and ice cream was the perfect emotional-repair food to keep them going.

She picked up the bowls, about to carry them into the living room, when her phone rang. She groaned — stupid tele-marketers. She did like hanging up on them, though. "Yeah?" she answered, licking a smidgen of whipped topping from her manicured finger.

"Where's my wife at, you fat heifer?" Ronnie yelled from the other end. "I know you're behind this shit."

Shenique smirked. "Oh no, you didn't. I got your wife right here. Come get 'er. I dare ya. I got something for your ass when you get here, too" she said and cast a loving gaze at her Panther 100,000 Volt Stun Gun. Her father had gotten it for her last Christmas, it always sat by her purse, and she was just dying to try it out.

"Alright, look. I'm sorry," Ronnie said.

"You damn right you sorry. Sorry ass, no-workin', wanna be a big baller, motherfu–"

"Stop! I want to talk to my wife."

Shenique glanced into the living room. Beverly had just finished episode one hundred 23 of season twenty, and was about to start season twenty-one.

"She's in quarantine. On a strict diet of Oprah and self-esteem till she gets over you."

Beverly turned around, leaning over the couch. "Shenique, is that him?"

Shenique shooed at her like a fly. "Girl, you finish watchin' the show. You don't need to talk to him. It's only been a couple hours, Damn."

Beverly hit *pause* and went into the kitchen. She held out her hand. Shenique grunted and slapped it into her palm.

"Ronnie –" Beverly began.

"Bev!" he sounded relieved. "Baby, I know… I'm sorry –"

"Ronnie…" she tried.

"We can work this out. We can –"

"Ronnie –" she tried again.

"Let's get together and talk. I know it's late but—"

"Ronnie!" Beverly yelled. "I've had enough."

She could actually hear his lip tremble.

"But, baby… I love you. I'm trying to tell you, I'm getting a –"

"No! No, you don't!" Beverly said and stuck her finger into the bowl of Cherry Garcia. Shenique smiled and offered her a spoon. "You need me. You use me. You take advantage of me, and you're good at it. You're good at making me think you really care, but you don't care. How can you?"

"I was wrong," pleaded Ronnie. "I know I used you, but –"

"Let me guess," Beverly said as she scooped out a cherry. "You've changed."

"Yes! Yes, I've realized..."

Beverly stuck the cherry into her mouth. It was cold and chewy. Good stuff. "Ronnie, you're a thief."

Now she could hear his eyes pop out of his head. Actually pop.

"A WHAT?! Wait a minute! You knew I was using that money!"

"Not to gamble," Beverly said. "I was just watching Oprah, and she said –"

His teeth were grinding. Beverly could hear that, too.

"I don't care what Oprah said! Shut up about Oprah!"

"'Shut up'? You've changed, huh?"

"I didn't mean..."

"Don't look for me, Ronnie. I'm leaving town tomorrow."

Shenique took up her own spoon and sat on the counter. This was better than any daytime drama she'd ever seen.

"I have to get away from you," continued Beverly, looking at Shenique who was nodding at her enthusiastically. "I need to think stuff out. Figure me out."

"Bev, baby. Please don't. Just, look. Look out the window."

"The window?" Beverly asked and gestured to Shenique to open the drapes. They looked through the glass, and saw Ronnie soaking wet and illuminated by a half-lit Budweiser sign from the corner liquor store. It read only "__dw_iser".

Ronnie dropped to one knee, trying to be cinematically romantic and memorable. All he looked was pathetic.

"Let me see you before you go. I won't try to stop you, I promise. Please? Just let me explain."

Beverly tucked the phone underneath her chin and framed him with her fingers like a director telling the cameraman what shot she wanted. Ronnie was perfectly sorrowful and miserable — a wretched man-shell of his former self. "No, Ronnie," she said coldly, looking through the frame of her fingers. "I want to remember you just… like… this." The phone clicked like a camera shutter and the drapes shut.

"Oh no, you didn't!" he screamed. Ronnie picked up a rock, and threw it at the window. SMASH! The outer glass of the double paned window shattered! "REMEMBER ME LIKE THAT!" he yelled.

Shenique ripped open the curtains, lifted the window, and stuck her head out. "I'M CALLING THE POLICE! BREAK MY DAMN WINDOW! WHAT ARE YOU, TWELVE? YOU PAYING FOR FOR THIS WINDOW, PUNK ASS!"

"SNITCHES GET STICHES!!!" Ronnie yelled back from corner. "Call the police! I don't care!"

Shenique yanked the phone from an embarrassed Beverly. Beverly ran to the window. "Just go, Ronnie!"

"Beverly!... Baby!... Don't let her poison your mind against me! You know I love you."

Beverly thought a minute. Could he really be lying? Could she really have read him so wrong? She stilled her impulses and held back a tear.

"THEY ON THEY WAY!" Shenique yelled.

"RONNIE GO! I'M NOT BAILING YOU OUT!"

Ronnie grunted and stood there.

Shenique closed the window and yanked the curtains shut.

"That's alright. That's allll right," Ronnie mumbled to himself. "I'ma make you love me. Oh, yeah, you're gonna love me. Watch. And when I get you back…. I'm dumping you."

The "__dw_iser" sign flickered, casting Ronnie in a red, neon glow.

* * *

It was far too late for anyone to be dropping in unannounced. But, when Linda looked through the peephole and saw her soggy, haggard brother, she was

not at all surprised. She undid the chain, dead bolt, the other dead bolt, and cracked open the door.
Ronnie barged past her, leaving his mucky footprints on her freshly-waxed foyer.

"Some guy named Butter is after me," Ronnie said, exasperated. "Charles Schwab and Shenique are gonna have me arrested, and Oprah Winfrey hates my guts!"

"Have you been drinking?" Linda asked very nonchalantly.

"You're playing games?" Ronnie shrieked, water dripping into his face.

"I've got to get up early in the morning," Linda sighed and headed for the kitchen.

Jeff spun a mixture of piña colada in the blender, careful not to get any on his silken bathrobe.

"Hi, Ronnie," he said.

"Five grand. I need five grand. You gotta loan it to me."

"Is that all?" Linda asked, jotting a note on a small spiral bound and tossing it to Jeff. He caught it.

"I'm serious, Linda."

"You're always serious, Ronnie," she remarked then looked at Jeff. "What's he owe us?" she asked.

Jeff read a few figures and made a mental calculation. "Twelve thousand, one hundred.... and fifty."

"What, are you adding interest?" Ronnie spat.

"Of course," said Linda, as if it should have been obvious.

"That's cold."

"You want a holiday piña colada?" Linda asked. Maybe a drink would calm her brother down.

Jeff pushed 'puree' one, two, three times. "You've gotta go in a minute. We've got sex at ten o'clock."

"Are you guys deaf?" Ronnie exclaimed, pointing to both of them. "Your brother," he said to Linda, "and your brother-in-law," he said to Jeff, "is in trouble here. You wanna see me dead?"

Linda and Jeff exchanged a look, paused, and then looked back at Ronnie.

Linda cleared her throat. "You know, brother. I was watching Oprah –"

Ronnie lost what remained of his shit. "Argh! Shut up! Don't ever say her name around me again! It's a conspiracy; I swear to God, I'm a..." his voice trailed off. He sounded like a madman, and he knew it. "I need a place to sleep."

Ronnie turned on his heel. "I hope you two have great sex while your dead brother is in the guest room," he said and made his way down the hall.

At precisely 10:00, the bed springs above Ronnie room began to squeak weakly.

Ronnie stared up at the ceiling. "SOUNDS LIKE YOU'RE REALLY BANGING IT OUT UP THERE, JEFF!" he screamed as loud as he could. "NO WONDER SHE'S SUCH A MEAN, LITTLE WITCH!" The squeaking slowed. He laughed to himself at his ability to ruin someone else's night.

Linda's voice came through the heating duct. "Honey… honey, wait…." he heard Linda say. The squeak stopped completely now. "Let's try something I saw on Oprah..."

Ronnie flinched again. This Oprah chick was doing the most. She had something to say about everything. But then the sound of his sister's moaning came through the vent. WTF? Ronnie was pissed now. Slowly, her ecstasy filled his room like nightmare porn. And, just when it couldn't get any worse, it did. Jeff started to climax.

Ronnie stuck the pillow over his head. Maybe he could suffocate himself.

Oprah, he thought. Oprah, Oprah, Oprah. It was always Oprah.

Suddenly, Ronnie ripped the pillow from his head. A light bulb moment just flashed in his mind like a huge, day-time television goddess beacon.

A strange, sociopathic grin etched his face. The likes of which would make Hannibal Lector proud.

* * *

The line of people outside the Harpo Studios wrapped around the block. Twice. Studio personnel carried large bins labeled "Cell Phones." Each and every potential audience member placed their precious, cellular possessions inside. There was no sacrifice greater, and they were all too happy to make it. Ms. Winfrey, as stated so many times, hated them.

Inside her dressing room, Oprah sat before the mirror, loyally flanked by two of her trademark Golden Retrievers, Samson and Delilah. Oprah's stylist, Andres, a dapper man with even dappier hair, coaxed Oprah's coif into perfectly gelled alignment. Brittney Jones, the producer of the Oprah Winfrey

Show for five seasons running, stood behind her trying to take a tangle out of her own hair. Brittany never exploited Andres' hair styling techniques because a) no one cared what the producer looked like, and b) her hair was at the mercy of her forever-present headset.

"You've got a ton of thank you cards, flowers, and what-not from Teledosis," Brittany said, tapping her ear piece. The director was going ballistic over camera three's position as usual.

"Keep the cards. Put the flowers out for the audience." Oprah said. "I'd hate them to go to waste. You like these?" she asked, displaying a stunning pair of suede boots that graced her feet.

"They're gorgeous," Brittany remarked. "We're on in ten."

"Saw them this morning in the window at Chanel when I was jogging," Oprah commented, pointing to her toes, "I had to get them."

"All done," Andres said, patting Oprah's perfectly perfect hair.

"Thank you, Andres," said Oprah. She patted her dogs', and smiled at them. "Stay with Andres, pups."

Samson and Delilah wagged their tails in unison, synchronized happily, and in time with the jazz-fusion with a funky snare beat that began to play.

The Oprah Winfrey Show soundstage was like a cathedral. The audience erupted into deafening applause and the traditional standing ovation when she appeared. As Oprah made her way toward her mark, hands reached out to get the faintest touch –

even just her breeze – as she passed.

The red light on camera three lit.

Just behind it, Ronnie sat. He was the only one who sat during the standing ovation.

"John Gray is here, and he's going to be talking to us about Love Tanks," Oprah announced. "He'll be joining me and our special guest, Gregory Slipshank. Have you guys heard of them?"

More applause. Much, much more.

Except for Ronnie. He tugged on the sleeve of one of Jeff's dress shirts he borrowed that morning. The sleeves were too short, but Ronnie hadn't bought his clothes and was afraid to return to his apartment. He decided to roll them up instead.

Beverly tossed her hotel key onto the dresser and fired up the television. She had a photo shoot in an hour, but there was enough time to shower. She needed to wash away the events of last night – the image of Ronnie underneath the broken beer sign still etched in her mind.

The screen illuminated a skinny, Mars-and-a-hint-of-Venus author and therapist, John Gray. Next to him, the down-home southern boy, Gregory Slipshank, sat with his hands folded in his lap. Oprah looked on at them both, the concerned matron of all that graced the screen during the day time hours.

John leaned forward, his hands clasped as well. "You feel lonely because you never filled the friendship tank as a child," he said gently. Gregory nodded. "When your friend got caught in that bear trap and eaten by that bear, you stopped making new friends for fear that they, too, would likewise perish."

Gregory wiped away a falling tear. "I'm just so scared a'bears," he said in an endearing, Kentuckian drawl. "They look so cuddly, but they're so… so… viciousss." His 's' had a lisp.

Camera three framed a woman in Oprah's audience, crying and wiping away her own falling tears in empathy with Gregory and because of the sheer magnificence of being in the audience. It was a religious experience. The cameraman zoomed in on the woman's face. The guy next to her, constantly tugging at his shirt sleeves, was screwing up his shot.

"Do you still trap bears, Gregory?" Oprah asked soothingly.

"Well, ma'am, I live in Indiana now."

John patted Gregory's shoulder. "Well, good. There aren't any bears in Indiana. You'll be fine."

Gregory looked to Oprah with big, wet, hopeful eyes. "Just a ways from your farm, Ms. Oprah. Maybe we can be friends."

Oprah patted Gregory's lap then stopped. John was already patting his shoulder, so the gesture would come across the screen as weird. "John Gray, this has been amazing." She turned to camera one. "John's new book, *Children Are from Uranus*, is in bookstores now."

Jazz fusion with a funky snare began — this time with a saxophone accompaniment, Oprah's closing theme.

Beverly went to the bathroom and started the shower.

The grandest perk about being an Oprah Winfrey audience member was the legendary Q&A

afterward. Oprah was on stage, looking just like a real-life person, and should your raised hand be acknowledged, you were afforded ten to fifteen glorious seconds of Oprah's personal time. If the one hundred and forty million dollars Forbes reported as her income every year was correct — and it was, that meant she made $1,098,000 for each of the one hundred twenty-eight shows she did in a year. Each show took two hours, so she made over a quarter million an hour. That meant that fifteen second was worth about twenty-three hundred dollars. Television saints be praised.

Ronnie raised his hand.

A thin woman in a mousy brown dress was picked instead. She stood up, giddy. "Oprah, do you remember me from the elevator at Macy's? It was about ten years ago."

"Yes, I do," Oprah returned, knowing absolutely nothing about the thin woman. "You were wearing that… that..."

"Brown dress!" the woman chirped.

"Yeah, girl. I loved that dress."

The thin woman clapped her hands together and sat back down beside her friend. "I told you she'd remember me!"

Oprah pointed to a woman in the front row, the one reserved for the disabled. "Lady in red," she said.

"You've been an inspiration to me," the lady in red said through a little sob. "I just want to know if I can touch you. Can I have a hug?"

Ronnie rolled his eyes. *What a crock of shit.*

"Oh, you're so sweet. Of course you can," Oprah said and crossed to the red lady in the wheelchair. Oprah's bodyguard, Bud, all three hundred pounds of him, followed. You couldn't trust anyone.

Oprah and the red lady exchanged an embrace.

"Thank you so much," the red lady said, her little sob turning into a bigger one. "Can we have a picture?"

"Just one," said Oprah and knelt next to her. The studio photographer snapped their photo and every hand in the audience went up. Ronnie's went down. Choruses of 'me, too, please, me too' echoed throughout. Oprah chuckled humbly. "Sorry, just the first one that asks. I can't be here huggin' all afternoon. I've got another show to do."

The hands went down, disappointed. Ronnie's shot back up.

"Okay, one more," Oprah said and pointed to Ronnie.

She actually picked me, he thought and stood. "I came to find out something."

"Find out what?" asked Oprah smiling.

"If you can fix my life the way you fix everybody else's."

Oprah's smiled turned a bit patronizing, but in a sweet, caring way. "Well, what seems to be the problem?"

"As far as I can tell," Ronnie began. "You are."

Gasps arose from the audience. Oprah, however, remained stoic. She was, after all, a professional. And Bud was there.

Ronnie seized the opportunity. He'd never have another like it. "First, you tell my business partner she can do better than me. So, I lose my business, my house, my cars, and my money. Not to mention, a woman I loved. But, I guess I can thank you because at least I learned that she didn't really love me. Then, you tell my mother to throw me out of the house. My own mother. And, she does it. No hesitation. Now, I'm homeless. Then, you decide you like a toothbrush nobody else in the country likes. Now, I'm twenty thousand in the hole, and I've got a gangster after me. Then, you tell the one good person I had in my life — the one, good person — to dump me. So now, I'm here with you."

John Gray clasped his fingers in his lap. "You're the youngest of your family, aren't you?" he asked.

Ronnie shot him an icicle stare. "I'm not talking to you, JOHN!"

John stifled a chuckle. "Definitely the baby," he whispered under his voice.

"Come on with it, Ms. Winfrey," Ronnie continued. "You're rich! Smart. Powerful — enough to even ruin my life long distance. Your life goes just like you want it. What did I do wrong? What don't I get?"

Oprah took a thoughtful moment. *Poor man,* she thought. *His clothes don't even fit. How did he get in here?* "I know exactly what's wrong with you. It's the same problem I had for years."

The audience leaned forward. The world's greatest words of wisdom were about to be uttered. Already she'd taken more than a minute with Ronnie. This advice was worth upwards of ten thousand dollars now. It must be good.

"And, I know what you don't get," said Oprah.

"It took me a very long time to figure it out. But then, one day, the light came on and it was clear. And, without this one truth, someone like you – and you are just as I was – will never have peace. You will never regain your footing. You will never be happy." Oprah took a deep breath.

Like the rest of her audience, Ronnie was glued to her words. She had touched something inside him — something that felt like truth. Like hope. Knocking. Ready to deliver him from the hell his life had become.

Oprah continued, "That one thing—the that thing you need to understand more than anything else you've ever understood in your life—is simply this..."

And, it was at that precise, pivotal, life-altering moment that a cell phone rang.

The one in Ronnie's pocket.

Chapter Six

*T*he entire universe slowed as Ronnie unconsciously reached for his phone. It was like he was putting his hand through invisible molasses; the warnings from the audience went unheard as he casually pulled the phone out and checked the incoming number.

Oprah froze — her eyes opened to the size of quarters then narrowed. Her mouth dropped open in bewilderment. She threw her hands in the air, exhaled, turned, and left. Her ten thousand dollar per minute advice exited stage left without another word or thought of Ronnie.

It would turn out to be one of those robo-calls from an androidian secretary telling him he'd won a fantastic trip to the Bahamas, and all he had to do was attend a seminar at minimal cost.

Producer Brittany was in full high-speed, however, yanking the headset from her hair (which pulled out a substantial portion). "You can't have that in here! Get that away from him," she commanded her stagehand minions. They weren't paid to miss cell phones. "Someone's head is going to roll!"

"No, wait! I'm sorry!" pleaded Ronnie, clamoring from his mid-row seat to the stage. The linebacker of a bodyguard grabbed his elbow.

"Come with me, sir," Bud said with unnerving

politeness.

"You don't understand. Did you see? She left me hanging there. She's got to finish what she's saying."

"She asked me to finish it for her. 'You're banned,' she says. For life.'"

"What? That ain't right! How she gonna leave me hanging like that?"

"Don't know, bro, but you're gotta go," Bud replied as he tightened his ham hock of a hand around Ronnie's arm and escorted him out of the studio.

Bud took a small piece of delight shoving Mister Tight-Shirt-Rule-Breaker out of the Harpo Studios doors.

"For life," Bud smirked before shaking his head in pity and tsk-tsk-ing Ronnie. He spun his massive frame around and went back inside.

Ronnie was about to protest, but there was no one around to help him, not that anyone would listen — not anyone here, anyway. The wrapped-around-the-block line was still there, anxiously awaiting the second show of the day.

A network page breezed past him and proceeded to hand out flyers to the awaiting Oprah Hopefuls.

"Ladies, free passes to see Oprah tomorrow at the Women's Conference," she announced like a herald.

Ronnie hung back. His Spidey-sense was tingling. He strolled down the line, casual as hell and took note of the words on which he was eavesdropping.

A beautiful Korean woman read her flyer and rolled her eyes. "Do you believe this crap? This is the fifth time I've been here, and I still haven't gotten any good gifts," she complained.

"My neighbor came the other day and got all of Oprah's Favorite Things," an elderly man in an *I Heart Oprah Winfrey* shirt proclaimed with an air of pride.

The woman next to him laughed. "That's nothing. My girlfriend came two years ago and got a trip to the Bahamas. And new breasts!"

"What about this conference thing tomorrow?" a pimply teenager asked her equally pimply mom. "We going?"

"She won't give away anything there," pimply mom said and crumpled up her flyer. She tossed it into a wire trash can which read *Keep Chicago Beautiful*.

Ronnie bit down on the inside of his cheek and kept his full, undivided attention. He stood beside the trash can ready to defend his new territory like a bull elephant if necessary. Ronnie needed that flyer like a drowning man needs a life preserver. When the hell were they going to let those people inside? He couldn't be spotted digging out a flyer from the trash can. Hell, the Winfrey militia probably already had their satellites trained on him. He could not take any chances.

Salvation arrived in the form of the Wheelchair Lady. She'd already constructed a handsome cardboard sign that read:

"The Wheelchair Lady – As Seen on the Oprah Winfrey Show. Photos - $1.00"

People in the audience queue surrounded her,

dollar bills peeling off right and left.

Ronnie side-stepped closer to the trash can, slowly reached his hand inside, not watching, and felt around for the discarded flyer. He landed on a banana peel first and what he hoped was not a fully loaded Huggies before he found it.

He uncrumpled his treasure. The first eight words made his blood run cold.

See and Hear Oprah Winfrey Live – Women Only

Now, that was going to be a problem.

* * *

Beverly pulled out the last shirt from her suitcase. She hated unpacking, especially unpacking in a hotel room. She had her own apartment, dammit.

"I'm not as bad as the guy with the beard," she said to her phone. It was on speaker.

"You're his opposite." Shenique's voice sounded as though she was talking on a tin can. "He avoids relationships. You cover yourself in them. Mark, Ronnie... as long as it's a warm body, and it gives you something to think about other than yourself."

"I wonder what Mark's doing now?" Beverly asked then came to an instant, sad realization. "Wow," she admonished herself.

"It's okay," Shenique said. "Be alone for a while. Get to know yourself. You might like you."

Beverly sighed and folded a sweater into the dresser. "I wonder if he's still..." she thought aloud

then caught herself. "Sorry," she said. And closed
the drawer.

* * *

The Chicago Hilton was the coveted site for
Oprah's Women's Conference for six years now. And,
the hotel staff had learned to loathe it. The halls
would be crammed, the elevators, dining room, and
banquet room stuffed stem to stern with the hapless
and the lovelorn. They were an aggressive mob, the
Winfrey Devoted. And, it didn't help that Ms.
Winfrey's camera crew was setting up in the main
lobby. The crowd was already growing to biblical
proportions.

This year, the award for the Most Hapless and
Lovelorn would definitely go to the one currently
stumbling her way to the check-in desk. She was
awkward, flailing around like a giant penguin with a
gimpy flipper. Yet, she was determined. Ronnie
struggled to maintain even the slightest bit of balance
in the horrible red pumps he'd purchased at the
Goodwill and jammed his feet into, despite them
being two sizes too small. Still, at least he managed
to coordinate the shoes with a blue business pants suit
and red blouse with a flared '70s style wide collar.
The business suit helped him maintain a small bit of
dignity in the otherwise humiliating uniform. He had
originally thought of being a flat-chested woman, but
the pants suit needed more convincing. He opted for
a C-cup and went with Play-Doh for filler and a more

realistic bounce per ounce. The big, floppy red hat though — that was to cover the sad, used, and obviously fake wig of long curls. Foundation helped hide his beardline, and he'd hoped the matching red lipstick would distract if the foundation failed. The final adornment, a pair of fashion shades that turned out to be Gucci knockoffs. He actually looked kind of hot…as long as he was standing still.

Ronnie spotted his quarry, there, in the middle of cameras, lights, and those funny umbrella reflectors whose purpose no civilian really understood. It wasn't terribly difficult for Ronnie to muscle his way through the weaker gender. He shoved aside one smaller woman after another with a mild grunt or falsetto "S'cuse me." After all, his mission was far more important than any one of the fan girls here today.

Except for one particular fan girl — twice Ronnie's size and twice his determination, dressed in another polyester pants suit, but this one with pearls. Her close-shaven gray hair indicated that she was most likely the husband in her relationship. And when Ronnie tried to push his way around her, he was met by her sharp elbow in his ribs.

"Slow your roll, chick," the polyester person said in a voice that sounded like she gargled with gravel. "We all wanna see the queen."

"It's important," Ronnie returned, a bit deeper than he intended. He cleared his throat and thumped his chest before taking it up an octave, "It's important," Ronnie said, "I've gotta talk to her."

Ronnie attempted a quick right, even in heels he could out-maneuver this linebacker he thought, but he was sadly mistaken.

Instead, Pearls and Polyester clotheslined him with the swift agility of a MMA warrior. Ronnie got to his feet, an accomplishment in itself, and gave Pearls and Polyester a girl-slap on her head — her very thick, very hard head.

Polyester glared at him with the heat of a thousand suns. "Nobody hits me like that unless she's dressed in black leather," she growled and bashed Ronnie right in the kisser.

Ronnie wheeled his arms and, only through a supreme act of divine intervention, stayed on his feet. He wanted to punch her back, but he could never seriously hit woman — even as a woman. "Cunt," he muttered.

"What?" Pearls and Polyester wasn't going to let him get away with that either. She sprung forward — amazing for her size — and landed on top of him.

A crowd gathered to watch the battle of the pantsuits and see Ronnie get his for having pushed past them. They cheered for Pearls and Polyester.

Oprah's cameraman turned his lens at the commotion for a second, but Oprah kept moving. She was too far away to notice the commotion. The cameraman refocused on Oprah and got back to business.

Meanwhile, it was a pile-up of estrogen. Ronnie, somehow, managed to wiggle his way out from the bottom. He got to his feet and beat a hasty retreat — as hasty as he could, given he was starting to go numb beneath his ankles.

"Oh no, you don't," Pearls and Polyester snarled. She freed herself from the heap and gave chase.

Ronnie fled to the elevators and pressed the

button. Again... and again... and again... and why did he think that would work? Why does anyone think repeated pressing works? It is one of the greatest unsolved mysteries of all time.

Pearls and Polyester grinned. Her prey was cornered. "It's you and me, baby. Let's go."

Ronnie turned to face her and dropped his falsetto like an anvil. "Get away from me, lady," he said, deep and burly. "I don't want to hurt you. I know karate." He turned slightly sideways and Namaste-ed.

Pearls and Polyester curled her lip in a smile. "You talk tough for a guy in pumps. Let's see what you got." Her voice was even deeper than Ronnie's.

Ronnie hit the buttons more, but it was too late. Polyester landed a left to his jaw, a right to his abdomen, and doubled him over like a cheap suit. Ronnie filled his lungs and flew erect. His floppy hatted head connected into Pearls and Polyester's jaw accidentally. The impact sent her back. Way, way back... to the wall... she's gone!

Ding.

Finally, the stupid elevator thought Ronnie, reaching his hands up to his throbbing, throbbing head before wandering off down the hall with vertical Play-Doh breast, looking for a place to get himself together.

The elevator opened and a woman in her mid-fifties, but trying to cover it up with thousands in Botox treatments, gasped when she saw the polyester woman laid out like a rug. "Lloyd?!" she screamed and ran to his side. "What are you doing in my clothes?"

The other passenger from the elevator exited,

took a moment to ponder the insanity she witnessed and thought it best to move along. Beverly didn't know what she could do to help, anyway. And besides, she'd heard rumor that Oprah had already arrived.

The gods must have been smiling on Ronnie. He was too preoccupied with his crooked hat, splitting headache, and vertical breast to notice his estranged wife. What he needed was sanctuary. Sanctuary...

And, that could be found in the Ladies Restroom.

Ronnie found it outside the main conference room. It was unlike anything he'd ever seen — a Xanadu of everything plumbing, toilet, and eau de' parfume; vaulted ceilings, a chandelier, even a small bar serving champagne. Women were gathered around like a social club. A string quartet played Mozart. There were purple velvet couches and little chocolate desserts.

Ronnie heard the rumors of such a place existing. But it was like the Fountain of Youth or the Loch Ness Monster or Bigfoot. You never truly believed until you saw. He took a seat at a crushed velour vanity stool and immediately adjusted his boobs back to true. Ronnie opened his sequined clutch – a Goodwill bargain at fifty cents – and took out a lipstick and mascara. He wasn't very practiced in their application and decided to copy what the two women next to him were doing. They each wore name tags, *Hello, My Name is Pauline*, and *Hello, My Name is Stephanie*. Stephanie had drawn a smiley face on hers.

Stephanie swept her Great Lash wand across

her eyelashes. "I hear she's going to talk about living one's best life."

Pauline pushed her breasts up and achieved a little cleavage, but when she released her boobs, they drooped like a couple of sad socks. "Wonderbra smunderbra. These tits don't tolerate tamin'," she said. "Gene didn't want me to come. The insensitive prick. He doesn't think running a home is a business."

"I know," Stephanie agreed. "Jim just wants me to wait on him hand and foot. Does he even know I have goals of my own?"

"Does he care is the question," said Pauline, as she reached for some Cotton Candy lip gloss. "You see the show the other day? I swear, I don't know why I stay married to him. It does nothing for me."

Ronnie stuck his mascara brush back in the tube. "Oh, you get plenty out of it," he replied, remembering his high register. Stephanie and Pauline turned to him, glaring. "Who's fooling who? You know us girls, as long as we're getting over everything's fine. But if we get the short end of the stick, it's 'something's wrong with this relationship'."

"What's your name, sweetie?" asked Stephanie.

"Ronnie… uh… Ronnia."

"Well, Ron ee aaah, mind your own damn business."

Pauline tapped Stephanie on the shoulder. "No, I've got this," she said and focused her attention on Ronn-ee-ahh the butt-in-ski. "There's something wrong when either partner in a relationship feels used. Agree?"

A restroom attendant with a tray of champagne flutes offered one to Ronnie. He took one and sipped, pinky finger raised like a true, classy dame.

"But it's no big deal until it's us girls," Ronnie proclaimed and wiped his mouth. We stay home, watch the soaps, and pretend to work hard while the man slaves at work. Then, we complain he's not romantic or he's insensitive and somehow manage to make him feel guilty about it. Let's face it, if it's the other way around, the man's a worthless bum."

Both Stephanie and Pauline stared ice cubes at the traitor sitting next to them. "First of all," Pauline began. "I only watch two soaps, and I run the house. As far as my husband is concerned, he's got a cushy job where his secretary does all his work, and he does three hour lunches."

"That's just like us women," Ronnie said and spun the tube of his lipstick. "We push out a baby and act like we deserve a Nobel Prize or something. You know lion prides? The females do all the work and the males just hang around and have sex all day."

"Sweetie, that's how it is everywhere," said Stephanie. "But at least the lion knows how to do it quick and get it over with."

Pauline snorted and reached up for a high-five. Stephanie slapped her palm.

"And, it's not like I'm faking it," Stephanie said. "Last week I'm screaming out my shopping list... *oh, oh, creamed corn! Oh, yeeesss, bagels!*" She took a breath. "And the idiot doesn't get it."

Ronnie shook his head. "See that's what I mean. Why not talk to him if there's a problem? Why make fun of him like this?" A funny lump raised in Ronnie's throat. "Then, one day you just up and leave and he has no idea why. Then, he spends the rest of his life taking out his frustrations on other people. Other women. And, the cycle goes on and on," he took a Kleenex from a silver dispenser on the counter and blew his nose hard.

Pauline and Stephanie exchanged a suspicious look, silently agreeing that they couldn't handle the emotions spewing forth from the strange, big, throwback Coco Chanel wannabe.

Over the hotel intercom, a feminine voice announced; "The conference is starting, ladies."

Every abled body in the restroom made a mass exodus for the door, leaving Ronnie alone, looking at his face, contemplating his thoughts. Real tears had formed and started melting his makeup.

"Dude, just cause you're dressed like a chick doesn't mean you gotta get all menstrual," Ronnie said, sniffling. "Pull it together, boy." He produced an eyeliner from his clutch and went to apply its inky magic. He stabbed himself in the eye, instead. "Now, look what you did. What's wrong with you? Look at you. You're a mess," he blubbered. "Hold it together. Be a man!"

Ronnie slapped himself across his face and snapped himself out of it.

It was Standing Room Only in the Hilton Ballroom where Oprah stood at a podium. Thousands of eyes were trained only on her. The queen of daytime.

"Pearl Bailey said, 'You never find yourself until you face the truth'," Oprah took a small, dramatic pause. "Yet, many of us hide from that truth. Painful truth. The truth of who we are. Of why we are the way we are."

Ronnie sat and listened. He took note of the throngs of people, the press, and the photographers. Quite a turnout. Many of them were scribbling notes or recording Oprah's wisdom on their phones, including Beverly, who sat, unnoticed by Ronnie, only two rows directly in front of him.

Beverly clicked her pen and shook it. Almost out of ink. She took a Chicago Bears pen from her purse – one that Ronnie let her borrow many, many moons ago – and sighed. She dismissed the irony and kept writing.

Across town at Legends, Butter was enjoying a rum and coke, sans the paper umbrella. The bartender, Henry, wiped out a glass. He looked as if he were trying to recall something.

"Ronnie Mitchell…" Henry said in his thick, Jamaican accent. He flipped his dreadlocks away from his eyes and kept wiping. "Ain't seen him in six months. Heard he married Shenique's best friend."

"Who?" Butter asked and signaled for another.

"Yah, I'm sure she know where him is," Henry said as he poured. "She come for Ladies Night, ya know. That be tomorrow."

"Tomorrow? Cool," said Butter and stuck a few cherries into his drink.

A pretty, young woman in a black mini-skirt and tight red blouse sat next to Butter. Butter looked her up and down and smiled.

The young woman looked him down and turned away.

Across the city, at the Hilton, another red blouse sat at another bar alone. The packed conference room, coupled with the truth, had grown too warm for Ronnie, so he had removed his jacket. Ronnie threw back his second shot of tequila, hoping to drown out the emotions that were overwhelming him. Just then, a baritone voice spoke from behind him.

"Excuse me. May I buy your next drink?" Bud the bodyguard asked.

Ronnie's eyes bulged. He recognized the voice and looked up and down the bar before facing what he already knew to be the worsening of his day, "I… I really shouldn't. I've had two." Ronnie pulled his hat down further and pushed up his 'Goochie' frames.

Bud signaled the barkeep. "Bartender? A double for the lady. I'll have a beer," Bud said as he sat next to Ronnie. This was a fine, fine big woman. Bud had a thing for Foxy Brown back in the day and this was his dream come true, "You here for the conference?"

Ronnie nodded, checked his boobs. They were still straight.

"I work for Oprah," Bud said, puffing up his substantial chest. "I can get you in to see her, if you like."

Opportunity knocks in the strangest of places at the strangest of times. It would be a hell of a risk, but one Ronnie was willing to take. "Really?" he said, escalating his octave another half-key. "What do you do?"

"I'm her bodyguard. Can't you tell?" Bud flexed his bicep nearing ripping through his suit jacket. Ronnie slowly reached out to Bud's arm and poked it with his finger.

"Why, yes, you are a big strong one," Ronnie said. "And, I would love to meet Oprah."

Bud grinned. Big and toothy. "I call her 'O'. I can arrange it."

The bartender placed another cocktail in front of Ronnie and a big schooner next to Bud. Ronnie took up his drink and promptly choked on it. Bud was running his ham hock of a hand down Ronnie's back and onto his ass. Bud squeezed. Enthusiastically.

Of all the nerve, Ronnie thought.

"We can go upstairs to my room, and I'll have her come over."

"Sounds like a plan," Ronnie squeaked.

Bud threw a wad of cash on the bar and extended his hand to the fair Ronnie. Ronnie gulped, grabbed his jacket and purse, took Bud's hand, and allowed himself to be escorted out of the bar.

A few booths down, Beverly finished off a virgin martini. She checked her watch and was about to get up to leave when a handsome man in a business suit and tie stopped next to her. Mark flashed his pristine, trademark smile.

"Well, Beverly Bunn-Jones-Bunn-Jones…Bunn," he said, smooth and cool.

Beverly looked as though she'd just had ice water thrown in her face. "It's Mitchell," she said, before admitting, "….Bunn. Well, soon to be Bunn again, anyway."

"You gotta be kidding me. Someone other

than me married you?"

That ice water turned instantly hot. Beverly felt the hairs on her neck stand up. "What brings you here, Mark?"

"You know me. My life is like that Michael Jackson song, 'got me working, working, day and night.'"

Beverly smiled. "Oh, yeah. I remember."

"You look good," he was being honest, not flirting. "Very good." Beverly appreciated the compliment. "And you?" he asked.

"The Oprah Conference."

Mark shook his head and condescended, "Still haven't figured out what you want outta life, uh?"

Beverly did, however, just figure out what she didn't want and was glad she no longer had —him . There would be no more hyphen Jones.

"Okay, that was wrong. If it makes you feel any better, I just broke up too," he added.

The unexpected humility disarmed Beverly. "Aww, boo. You mean someone besides me liked you?" She couldn't resist.

"Touché," Mark said and sat down with his ex, ex, ex-wife.

Bud the bodyguard's room was a nice single suite. Flowers and candles – prerequisites for any of Oprah's staff – lined the room. Ronnie felt as though he'd just walked into the proverbial lion's den, accompanied by the biggest lion of all. He may as well have been wearing raw meat.

"So, call Oprah," Ronnie said. "I want to

meet her right away.

Bud grinned. "There's time for that, sugar. Let's get to know each other first," said Bud and without warning, pulled Ronnie against his chest. The Play-Doh mushed between them.

Air escaped from Ronnie's lungs. He couldn't breathe. He shoved Bud away and stumbled in back of the couch. Bud's grin got wider. He liked the cat-and-mouse game.

"You move fast for a big guy," Ronnie complimented, as he turned to try to round out his fake breast.

"Fast, slow, however you like it, baby." Bud unbuttoned his jacket, approaching.

Ronnie leapt over the back of the couch. "It's cold," he said. "You should leave that on."

"It's gonna get hot real soon," Bud replied. Such the Casanova.

"Why don't we do this after we see 'O'."

"We've got plenty of time. Why ya playing hard to get?"

"I don't want to get got," Ronnie said and made an awkward dash around the couch again.

"You're my kind of lady," Bud remarked. He didn't even know this broad's name, but that only added to his admiration and need for conquest.

Ronnie grabbed a throw pillow and held it in front of him. "You might be surprised."

"Oh, you like surprises?" Bud asked and threw himself at Ronnie. He grabbed Ronnie and pulled him toward his lips. Ronnie struggled, but no dice. Bud's mouth pressed against his.

It was, without a doubt, the single grossest thing Ronnie ever experienced. He attempted to escape, but it was like being held in a big, breathing straight jacket. Bud pulled back and looked into Ronnie's moist, watering eyes.

"This time, give me some tongue," Bud suggested.

Death would be better. Ronnie drove his knee into Bud's groin, doubling him over.

"How can you treat a woman like that?" Ronnie shrieked and, driven by testosterone, grabbed Bud's head and slammed it into his knee. Repeatedly.

"No means no, no, no!" Ronnie yelled.

On the last 'no', Ronnie let Bud's head go. Bud fell backwards onto the coffee table, crashing against a vase of lovely, pink carnations.

"You know, being a woman is hard enough without assholes like you," Ronnie said calmly as he re-rounded his tits and smoothed his wig. He checked his lipstick and mascara in the mirror. All systems go. He stepped over Bud, crossed to the door, opened it, and caught his heel on the carpet on his way out. He stumbled but righted himself. Ronnie took in a few deep calming breaths.

The elevator bell sounded from down the hallway. The doors opened, revealing Oprah, Brittany the Producer, and several remaining members of the entourage.

Ronnie gasped in excitement. "Oprah!" he cried. "Oprah!" He started running toward her, but his heel that had caught on the carpet snapped in half. He tumbled forward, unable to stop himself this time, and crashed head first into a giant palm pot. He was knocked out, cold.

"Oh, my God!" Oprah ran toward him. The

poor dear!

    In the lobby bar, Bev and Mark had warmed up to each other as they shared glasses of red wine. "Then two months ago, I won the Clio," she said.

    "Damn. Wow! Congratulations, Bev!" Mark raised his wine glass to her.

    "And, now I'm rethinking everything."

    "Everything?" Mark asked, hopefully.

    Beverly eyed her ex, ex, ex, knowing exactly what he meant. She didn't answer. They were having a good time. Why ruin it?

    "I mean, since you're rethinking everything… you still think I'm cute?"

    "Like a teddy bear," she said with intentional ambiguity.

    It worked. Mark had no idea what that meant but kept moving forward with his optimism, "I'm in town through Christmas. But say the word and I can postpone my travel… indefinitely. I'm staying here. Room 810. Can I get you a cab?"

    Beverly shook her head no.

    "You're here, too?" Mark sat back down.

    Was this going to happen again? Beverly heard that familiar warning bell ringing in her head. She was on a bad road. She needed to remember, but he was so cute tonight. *Why did we break up?* She asked herself, as if on cue.

    "I know what you're thinking. I want you to know I forgive you for the candlestick." Mark began.

    Aha! Everything was fresh again. "I never hit you with a candlestick, Mark!" shouted Beverly, livid. How dare this guy? "And I don't appreciate you telling everyone I did!"

The bitch was crazy as shit. It was the only possible answer. "I want you to know something," Mark said through his teeth, not appreciating his graciousness being shoved back in his face. "You'll never keep a man. You know why? Because you are fucking insane. Have a great life," he said as he stood and left.

Beverly shot up from the booth. "Mark, I want *you* to know something."

Mark stopped and turned around.

"Someone may like you," Beverly's chest was heaving. "Someone might love you. But, you are not, nor have you ever, ever even remotely been… cool."

Mark deflated like an old balloon. Beverly smiled and took up her purse.

"You have a great life, too," she wished him and left the bar.

Ronnie didn't know how much time had elapsed. Only that it was enough for him to be nestled in Oprah's arms on her couch in the presidential suite. He was dressed in a fluffy white hotel robe, the initials CH embroidered in gold thread. Ronnie turned his head and saw Brittany draping his green dress and wig on a chair. Fear shot through him, but Oprah continued stroking his head, lovingly.

"I'm so sorry," Oprah said to him. "If I'd known you were this desperate, I would have overlooked the cell phone thing."

Tears sprang into Ronnie's eyes. "It's been so hard, O."

"Take your time," Oprah whispered. "Tell O all about it."

He did. Ronnie didn't remember actually speaking or how much detail he went into, but when he was finished, Oprah was looking at him with a genuine mixture of empathy and shock.

"That's terrible!" she said. "I feel terrible. I can't believe I put you through all that. Of course. I'll stop using that toothbrush and put in some good words for you." Oprah pointed to Brittany. "Prepare a press release – Oprah electrocuted by her Sonic Motion Toothbrush."

Oprah ran her hands through her hair, mussing it. She bugged her eyes, looking very much like she'd put her finger in a light socket. Brittany readied a camera and took the picture.

The next thing Ronnie knew, he could see the Chicago Tribune's front page. The headline…

Shocking Side Effects of Sonic Brush!

Even Business Weekly got on board, their leading article stating *Teledosis Stock Plummets.*

Ronnie looked up at Oprah. She smiled down at him and caressed his face.

"Set up a show on Chicago's Best Looking Men," Oprah said to Brittany. "Put Ronnie here on."

Brittany began to write furiously on her notepad.

Oprah's eyes were warm and soft and wonderful. Her hands, equally so.

"We'll get her back to you," she cooed. "By the way, I give away ten percent of what I make every month. You think you could use some extra cash, honey?"

Ronnie nodded but his head was starting to hurt. Oprah's caresses turned into pats. Hard ones. Over and over and over…

Oprah's attempts at reviving the woman weren't working. She was still unconscious, but at least, she was breathing. It took a Herculean effort to get her into Oprah's suite and onto the couch. Oprah wondered just where Bud disappeared to, as they certainly could have used his help in this situation. Thankfully, Oprah's camera person was big on working out.

Brittany tapped her headset. "An ambulance is on the way," she said.

"This is just so horrible," Oprah remarked. She patted the woman's face one last time – the poor thing obviously had trouble with facial hair. "What a strong jawline, though. It's like Maria Shriver's. It's a Kennedy jawline. I'd love a jawline like this," Oprah sighed. "Here, help me get her shoes off."

Oprah and Brittany each took hold of a shoe and pulled. And yanked. And grunted. It was like playing tug-of-war with a rhinoceros. Oprah grabbed firm hold of Ronnie's broken heel and threw herself back. Ronnie's feet – complete with tattered stockings – were exposed.

"Oh, gramma, what big feet you have," Oprah turned to Brittany, still unable to remove the shoe she was struggling with. "It must be hell for her to find shoes. They're at least two sizes too small. And this wig…Jesus. Oh, sister, I see why you chased me down. Schedule her for our next make-over show."

Brittany nodded and made notes. The photographer snapped a few pictures.

"No wonder you fell, honey," Oprah spoke to the unconscious Ronnie. "She must have wanted these shoes bad. I know how it feels, girl. Just had to have these red pumps. Almost died for these shoes. It's just not worth it, sweetie."

Oprah positioned Ronnie's head on her lap. "I'll just let her rest," she said as she tried to fix the wig back in place on Ronnie's head. She gave up and just covered it with the hat. Oprah began reading a book titled Lunar Options by T.R. Locke. "This is so good," she said. "It's got black people running around on the moon. Put this in the Book Club."

Ronnie snoozed in Oprah's lap.

Outside, an approaching siren wailed then stopped.

The cavalry had arrived.

Ronnie came around, slowly. He awoke not to find himself in the arms of daytime's greatest star and his life completely fixed but strapped to a gurney in the back of a bouncy ambulance.

He couldn't make out the conversation of the EMTs. Only that it seemed they were arguing about the shortest route to take to the hospital. Ronnie couldn't go to a hospital. The second they wheeled him into the emergency room, they'd find out. There would be cell phone videos of him all over the internet. Ronnie Mitchell in drag would go viral. This was not an option.

Ronnie tried to free himself but the straps were tight, too tight. He started rocking himself back and forth. The gurney wheels were only held in place by small bumpers, and knowing the amount of money the city invested in its emergency vehicles, Ronnie remained confident that his plan at escape would work.

It did — all too well.

The gurney flew at the ambulance doors and smashed them open. Ronnie and his gurney ejected from the vehicle. Like James Bond but without the suave.

Horns blasted. Streets were crammed with Christmas pedestrians, each of them jumping out of the way of this bizarre medical missile. Tires screeched, but one particularly large Buick with bad brake pads couldn't react in time. It side-swiped Ronnie and his gurney, sending them off into a darkened alley where a drunken Santa Claus – straight off his shift at Bloomingdale's – staggered.

"Dreidel, dreidel, dreidel, I made it out of clay," Santa sang. "Dreidel, dre –"

Wham! Ronnie's gurney knocked Santa on his ass.

"Manishevitz!" Santa shouted, getting back to his feet. His blurred vision focused on Ronnie, strapped down on the bed. "There is a god," Santa said and took a swig from his brown bag.

"Hey, Santa," Ronnie gasped, out of breath. "Give me my Christmas gift early this year."

"Your gift? I thought you were my gift. Mrs. Claus tied up," Santa said through a sneer. "I was about to show you my north pole." Ronnie ignored the pervert and struggled against the straps. "Ah, okay," Santa reluctantly consented. He released Mrs. Claus from her confinement. "Don't see what the rush is, honey."

Ronnie stood up, towering over Santa like a giant, mutant elf.

"Oh..." Santa remarked. "You're a lotta woman," he said, noting that Mrs. Claus' flat breasts were crooked. "Whatcha got there?"

Santa reached out to Ronnie's chest. Ronnie slapped his hand away.

"Back off, Santa!" Ronnie growled deeply, "I had a bad day." Ronnie then noticed the man's shiny, black boots. "How much for those?" He pointed at Santa's feet.

"How much for what?" Santa asked. He did not remember Mrs. Claus having such a deep voice.

"The boots. I need the boots," Ronnie said, not having time for this. He switched back to his falsetto, "Here, take the bed for the boots. You don't want a lady catching cold do you?"

Ronnie lifted Santa onto the gurney, took off his boots, and fluffed the pillow for him.

"Strong, too. What a woman! You kinda look familiar," Santa said. "Do I know you?" Drunk Santa laid back on the gurney and folded his hands over his belly.

It was the same Santa Ronnie had hired the previous year to pass out the bonus checks at Mitchell-Nagy. Ronnie recognized him but certainly didn't want Santa to make the connection. "No you don't," Ronnie was firm. "Thanks for the boots. Get some rest, Santa."

"Okay, honey," Santa replied and drifted off to sleep.

Ronnie headed off down the alley in Santa's boots, massaging his throbbing head.

Chapter Seven

*O*prah sat at her dressing room vanity waiting for Andres the hairdresser. The lights surrounding the mirror shone down at her like a dozen spotlights glaring down at the newspaper she held. She was front-page news again. Big, attention-grabbing font announced *Oprah Saves Fan at Women's Luncheon.*

Beneath the article, in the lower-left corner where statistics show readers rarely look, the Indian Summer was on its way out, and a significant snowstorm was forming to take its place as the top weather story.

Brittany adjusted her headset, and as customary, it got stuck in her hair. She'd be glad when the humidity finally left. It made her hairdo even more frizzy than usual. She noticed a Ralph Lauren bag on the counter. "What's that?"

"I had Ralph send over a pair of red pumps in her size. I was going to surprise her at the hospital this morning, but she never made it." Oprah continued reading, "They think the doors opened on the ambulance and she fell out."Oprah shook her head. "No one saw a gurney fall out of an ambulance? Impossible. We need to find her, Britt."

"Well… I think Jimmy took a picture of her. For the make-over show."

Oprah's face lit brighter than the bulbs around

the mirror. "Put it on the air," she said.

Beverly finished dressing in her hotel room. As she put on a bracelet Ronnie gave her in Gary, she got an idea. She examined it, along with a pair of ruby earrings he'd given her and, finally, her engagement ring. She checked the notes she'd written at the conference. One read: *Declare your independence*. That's exactly what she would do. She exited her room and waited at the elevator with the same two women Ronnie had debated in the restroom.

"I'm sure it was her. Same pantsuit, same fake tits," Beverly heard one say.

"I think she's a T," the other added. "Shoulders were just a bit too broad to be a broad, right?"

The women snickered as the elevator opened. Lloyd (formerly Pearls and Polyester), now dressed as a man with a bandage beneath his chin, exited arm and arm with his wife speaking to him, "Dr. Phil says he can see you on Tuesday or Friday afternoons for an hour each week. He thinks he can get you cured in two years…"

On Michigan Avenue's Magnificent Mile, a cool breeze blew back Beverly's scarf. She smiled, but it was bittersweet. There was something about Ronnie, as much of an ass that he was, that she missed. He was so much better than Mark — even with the thieving and lying. Nonetheless, she was determined to follow Oprah's advice to declare her independence from him.

The light on the corner flashed to Don't Walk. Beverly stopped directly in front of the window that still displayed the coveted red leather jacket. She smiled again, this time without the bitter sweetness. That's it!

A green man replaced the order not to walk, and Beverly took it in stride, literally. Her gait took on the cadence of a strut as she crossed the intersection. She didn't stop at the coffee shop for her traditional morning latte. It was time for a change, sure enough.

Had Ronnie not been so depressed, he might have lifted his head long enough to notice Beverly breezing past his window. Instead, he blew the steam off his Tall French roast, scratched his face – his five o'clock shadow had about ten extra hours of growth on it, and it poked through his make-up like a bizarre, itchy porcupine.

A young hipster – complete with lumberjack beard and porkpie hat – couldn't help but stare at the tranny sitting at the counter and talking to her coffee. The hipster was tolerant to all forms and walks of life, race, creeds, and sexual orientations, but sometimes, weird was weird, and you just had to look.

Ronnie felt the hipster's stare on the back of his neck. "Oprah stole my shoes," he yelled aloud to no one in particular. "Got me in these damn boots… Santa Claus and bodyguards all trying to have sex with me."

The whole restaurant stirred and made sure Ronnie made no sudden moves. He quieted down again, and they went back to their chatting.

The hipster nodded. Best not to aggravate the aggravated. There were news reports every day about somebody losing their shit over a variety of reasons. This situation didn't have to be headline worthy, and the lady was already on edge, obviously. What was stranger is that she was suddenly drawn to the TV above the counter. It was broadcasting one of those financial adviser firm commercials. The transvestite in the blue suit and red blouse seemed to be taking personal offense to it.

Harry Robinstone looked awkward in front of the camera. But the director of The Bartlesby Funds commercial thought that would bring a human element to the advertisement. Harry sat up, straight and rigid, and told the world that Bartlesby Funds was number one.

Ronnie scowled. "You wouldn't be shit without me," he snarled and hurled a package of Sweet-N-Low at the screen. It didn't get very far, lacking in the aerodynamic department. Ronnie, though, took it personally. He hung his head.

Wishing he could think better of it, the hipster gently tapped him on his shoulder. Ronnie spun around, creasing his brow as the young man with groomed, yet somehow unruly, facial hair handed him a business card.

"I understand these people can help," the hipster said, then turned to leave. He'd done his good deed for the day and had no desire to keep pumping good vibes into his Karma tank. Ronnie looked as if he was one click away from completely losing it.

The card was a soothing powdered pink – the sort of shade they used to paint jail cells. The color was rumored to have calming influence. Comic Sans letters in a slightly darker tone spelled out "**Way of the Light Shelter**."

Ronnie's brow creased. He didn't need no stinking shelter.

Did he?

Ronnie didn't have time to think of the possibility. His phone started to ring.

"Hello..." he answered, troubled by the sound of his own voice. It sounded like a shadow.

"Ron?" Ted said from the other end. "Ron, some big guy was here looking for you." Ted had been peeking through the living room curtain all morning. A sinister looking black Range Rover was still parked across the street. "And some goon's been outside ever since." Ted closed the curtain tightly. "You're serious, Ron. You're in trouble."

"No shit, Sherlock," Ronnie returned.

"Whatever you do, don't come back today," Ted said. "I'll see what I can do."

The screen on Ronnie's phone said Call Ended.

He picked up the Way of the Light card and read the address. It was down State Street, next to a pawn shop.

Beverly stood in front of the pawnbroker's counter shifting her weight from one foot to another. This was how she planned to declare her independence.

The pawnbroker pulled the loupe from his eye and squinted at the ring. Then, he squinted at Beverly. "Sure you want to part with these?" he asked with an edge of tired sarcasm.

"We're not together anymore," Beverly explained. "Why not trade this in and get something I really want? It's just tying me to him, you know?"

"Uh-huh."

"I figure I'll end up getting something out of this, after all," Beverly went on explaining. Even though she didn't know why. The pawnbroker, she was sure, had heard this before — a lot. "It'll take some of the sting out of all he's done to me," she pressed.

"Sure, sure," the broker said and brought out his ticket pad. "I'll give you a hundred bucks."

"A hundred bucks? Look at the size of that diamond," Beverly said as she pointed. She grabbed the bracelet and held it to his eye. "Look at those beautiful rubies."

The broker sighed. "You mean cubic zirconia."

Beverly's face fell. "Cubic zirconia? The rubies are cubic zirconia?"

"No, the rubies are melted stop lights," the pawn star offered. "Don't get me wrong," he continued. "This is wonderful work. Whoever did it was an expert."

Oh yeah, Ronnie was an expert, alright, at being a son-of-a-bitch. Beverly snatched up the ring, bracelet, and earring. "Thank you," she said, feeling her temper simmering in the pit of her stomach. "Merry Christmas."

Beverly stormed out of the shop, the little bells jingling behind her.

A second earlier, she would run right into the

object of her anger, who was now entering the Way of Light Shelter, little silver bells jingled above the door as he did.   It was an average refuge, sparse and ratty, and smelled like Lysol and old mops. A plastic Christmas tree sat in the corner, frocked by assuredly flammable white fleece — only half its lights worked. An equally sad menorah was next to it – half its gold plating long since chipped away.

Ronnie had only gotten two steps inside when he was approached by two of the mission's representatives — two of the whitest young men on the planet: white shirts, white teeth, and matching orange pants. They looked like creamsicles.

"Come in, sister. Enter. The light loves --"

"I'm not a sister," Ronnie said in his shadowy voice. "I need new clothes."

The blue eyes of both Creamsicle boys went wide. This man's voice was deep and throaty and a whole lot like the Blood God Hakkar the Soulflayer in their World of Warcraft game. The first boy clutched his Bible and smashed Ronnie over the head with it.

"Repent, vile spirit! Come out of her!" he shrieked.

It was the wrong place and wrong time for that particularly form of exorcism. Ronnie had had enough, and this kid was about to be repaid for the last 24 hours of hell. Ronnie clocked the dude on the jaw and knocked him out cold.

"Brother Maximus!" yelled the second boy. "Help!"

Immediately, Brother Maximus – all six foot five, Arnold Schwarzenegger circa the 80's of him – appeared. His face was soft and kind. But he could bench press a Volkswagen.

"A demon has this woman," the boy said in a shaky, high-pitched voice that never quite found its way out of puberty. "We tried casting it out, but it attacked Brother Chris! I think it's a demon spawned of alcohol… and crack!"

"Hey, he hit me first," Ronnie defended and instantly found himself two feet off the ground. Brother Maximus had him by the throat. Ronnie fought to get free, but his effort failed to even shake the arms of the mighty Maximus.

"By dah power of dah light..." Brother Maximus chanted. "I command you…. come out!"

On the word "out", Brother Maximus flung Ronnie across the floor. Ronnie slid on his ass until he smashed into a green tile wall.

Brother Maximus moved in to check on the progress of the exorcism.

Ronnie saw him coming but couldn't move. Ronnie grasped his throat and tried to catch his breath.

"Sister?" Brother Maximus asked gently. "Are you restored?"

Thinking fast, Ronnie returned to his upper-register. "Yes," he croaked in an alto-soprano. "I'm fine now. Thank you. I just need to rest."

Brother Maximus smiled down at him and offered his hand.

The sound of Beverly's heels echoed through the hallway of the agency. She was a woman on a mission, god damn it, and she would not be denied.

Hector looked up from his paperwork,

surprised to see Beverly stomping toward him. She never stomped like that.

"Did you forget you're on vacation?" he asked.

"Let's get started on the next shoot," Beverly shot back.

"Um, okay..." Hector cleared his throat. "But, you know it's Modela, don't you?"

"Indeed I do."

Beverly continued down the hall to the studio. Her footsteps growing louder.

She flung open the door and saw Modela sitting with her back to her, primping her already flawless hair and nails, make-up, and wardrobe.

"Do not ever keep me waiting again!" Modela warned to whoever was behind her.

"You'll wait as long as it takes," Beverly said and strapped on her Nikon.

Modela turned around and took in a quick breath. "You!" She stood up and put her hands on her hips in her wonted look of prima-donna defiance.

"Sit down and shut up," Beverly retorted. She started setting the lens.

Modela did as she was told.

A grin etched on Hector's face. He'd never seen that sort of Beverly before and he kinda admired it.

Ronnie carried his assigned pillow and blanket to his cot in the Way of the Light woman's dormitory.

It was a walk reminiscent of all those prison movies, where the rookie arrival looks about his or her new surroundings. All that was missing was the warden.

"That's a pretty blouse," a young girl's voice said.

Ronnie looked down at a brown freckle-faced little girl. She offered him a smile, displaying her missing front teeth, then trotted off to join a group of her friends clapping along to *A sailor went to sea sea sea. To see all he could see see see...*

The cot sagged with Ronnie's weight. He felt like sagging, too, and not just in regards to his phony boobs. He pulled off his boots and accessed his new surroundings, feeling like the leading contributor on one of those hard-knock-life documentaries. There were so many women here, all in various stages of digression. Some had just started, obviously, as their clothes weren't as tattered as the Way of the Light veterans. But, what they all held in common was their humanity, as trodden on as it was.

One of the most trodden upon stepped up to him. She was on the other side of eighty and probably had more than a few lady of the evening decades under her belt where her breasts now hung.

"Yep," she said, noting where Ronnie's gaze had traveled. "It's what happens to double Ds after seventy years. They become extra tall Cs. Who says god doesn't have a sense of humor? Saves on bras, though," the old lady said as she pulled up the elastic band on her pants and tucked her tits inside. "Looks like you're on the way yourself, there, sweetie."

Looking down at his own chest, Ronnie saw his fake cleavage had descended yet again. He was getting tired of it. He sighed and pulled them back up into place.

"That's a neat trick," the old lady said.

"Something I saw on Oprah," Ronnie replied. "I'm Gretta, by the way."

Ronnie took Gretta's hand slowly. It was covered in age spots and skin that didn't fit anymore.

I need myself some boots like that," she said with a wink.

"Where are the showers, Gretta?"

"Straight down the hall, to the right."

Ronnie got up and began to make his way out of the dorm. "Thank you," he said.

"Hey, hon. You forgot your boots," said Gretta, pointing at them.

"Merry Christmas," Ronnie said and headed for the showers.

Gretta smiled – her front teeth were missing – and picked up the boots. They'd fit perfectly.

Down the hall and to the right — just like Gretta said. However, down the hall and to the left, were the Men's Showers. Ronnie paused not only because he was taken aback by the fact this place offered amenities for men, but also because he wasn't sure which shower he should choose. He picked the door on the left.

Before he went inside, he took note of a pile of donated clothes, shoes, and some paperback books that were displayed on a rickety card table. He picked through them, grimacing, as he felt like a stray dog looking for scraps. But the clothes were clean, and there were jeans that would fit — and shirts. He selected a gently used blue plaid shirt and a pair of

Levis. As he took the denim from the pile, a dog-eared book fell to the floor. He picked it up, about to set it back on the table, then stopped.

It was a John Gray self-help book. The one that weird-ass bear man afraid of commitment had been talking about on the forsaken Oprah Winfrey Show.

Ronnie tucked the book in with his "new" clothes. An idea was forming in his head.

Denise hid herself well behind stacks of legal briefs and her computer monitor. She twirled her hair and chewed her gum enthusiastically as she read the climactic portion of her romance novel. Francisco had just taken his shirt off again and was proposing to Rosa the handmaiden — so romantic. And, Francisco was the only blonde Italian –

The main line at the Hammond and Gray Law Offices rang.

"Hammond and Gray," Denise said, not really paying attention because Francisco had taken Rosa's hand in his. "No, sorry. He's gone for the holidays. Happy Christmas," wished Denise and sat on proverbial pins and needles because Rosa was covering her mouth and was about to give Francisco his –

The phone rang again.

"Hammond and Gray," answered Denise. She paid attention this time, as Rosa was taking a really long time saying 'yes'. She was going to say 'yes', wasn't she?

"Denise, it's me," Beverly said. She was in need of some emotional support, which was why she called Denise and not Shenique. Also, she was on edge. Her boss, Piatro Roget, was having a conversation with Modela. A very animated conversation involving Modela making a lot of over-exaggerated hand gestures and tossing of her incredible locks. Beverly knew this as her cubicle offered a great view of Piatro's office. Modela paced back and forth in front of the frosted glass.

"You're back already?" questioned Denise, hating to put her book down but Rosa was taking way too long in responding to Francisco. His knees must be hurting at this point.

"I don't know what's come over me, Denise. I think Mister Roget is being talked into firing me."

"He won't fire you," Denise said supportively.

Which was just what Beverly needed, as she'd mentioned. Especially now since Mister Roget was curling his finger at her. Modela had her hands on her hips and a smug expression — real smug.

"Oops. Gotta go. I'll talk to you later," said Beverly. She hung up and pushed her chair away from her desk. She took a quick glance at the one remaining picture of her and Ronnie at some long forgotten scenic location.

"I'll pray for you," Denise replied, unaware that Beverly already disconnected the call. Rosa told Francisco she needed time to think about it, and Francisco was devastated.

Beverly drew in a deep breath, held it, and entered Roget's office. Roget folded his hands across his desk, steepling his fingers together.

"Beverly, Miss Modela informs me a tiff has arisen betwixt thou deux?" asked Roget. His parents had left France when he was three months old, and it'd taken him a lifetime to perfect the Parisian accent.

"Yes... yes there has actually..." Beverly drew another pull of air, filling her lungs. "Actually, she's being an ass."

Modela's fake eyelashes almost fell of her lids.

Beverly liked the reaction and continued; "Apparently, she doesn't like the way I take her pictures." She pointed to the huge frame right behind Roget – the photograph inside was a double-exposed print of Modela holding the bouquet of one red rose in the midst of a dozen white buds. It was a masterpiece. "You, however, like it enough to hang it on your wall. So which one of us is crazy? Which one, Mister Roget?"

"You may call me Piatro," Mister Roget said.

Ronnie had secured a decently private computer station at the Harold Washington library. He scrolled down the Oprah Winfrey website and clicked on Archives.

The vid-clip of John Gray's heartfelt interview of the friendless bear man, Gregory Slipshank, waited for the user to click *play* which Ronnie did. The video played for quite some time without sound. Ronnie couldn't hear a word, wondered if computer was broken or the file corrupted, then realized the little speaker icon was red. He clicked on it.

"... just up the street from you, Oprah," Gregory said. "Maybe we can be friends."

Ronnie closed the tab, Googled the elusive Slipshank, G., and found him immediately — phone number, address, everything.

Time to initiate *Phase Two* of his plan.

It would take some time to bring that fruition, Ronnie mused. The guy was a hermit, a recluse.

Ronnie just hoped it wouldn't take some psychological act of God to get Gregory to meet with him for coffee.

As it turned out, it only took an offer of a half-caf Vente Vanilla, which Gregory slurped down happily, even twice as happy as new friend Ronnie Mitchell raised his triple shot espresso to him.

"This has sure been fun, Ronnie. Thanks for callin'."

"Hey, man, you touched me."

Gregory ran his finger against the inside of his cup, finding a little vanilla syrup left over. He sucked it off his pinky. "That John Gray got a way of getting down inside ya real personal like. I ain't never opened up like that."

"Well, because you did, I'm here now. So, yes, I'm willing to be your friend."

Lucky Gregory. Luckiest man in the whole damn world, if you asked Ronnie.

Gregory beamed. "Hey, friend, what say we go back to my place for some pool?"

Ronnie smiled. That was just what he was hoping for.

Gregory's truck plowed through a sudden heavy snow storm that developed around the south side of the city. *Safety First* wasn't Gregory's motto. Gregory barely seemed to care.

"Looks worse than they predicted," Gregory said over the grinding sound of his wipers. They weren't strong enough to dislodge the snow from the glass. "That's Oprah's farm there. Big, huh?" asked Gregory, pointing out his friend Ronnie's window.

"Sure is," Ronnie commented. The farm was more like a fortified medieval city. A stone wall surrounded the perimeter of the property – there was even an elevated guard house… complete with Guards.

"She's there now," said Gregory. "I know on accounta the gates is closed. I hear she's leaving in two days to holiday in Colorado."

Nice, thought Ronnie and stared in fascination as Oprah's Fortress of Solitude and A Shitload of Money disappeared into the distance.

Gregory's house was a tad more modest than his special neighbor's. But what it lacked in square footage, it made up for in weird. The living room was red, for starters. A dozen crimson lava lamps bubbled and oozed in perpetuity, casting everything in a vermillion mood light. The topper, however, was the inflatable kiddie pool in the center of the shag carpet.

Ronnie looked as if he'd run head first into a brick wall and, somehow, managed to retain consciousness. He'd rather not be conscious — not now.

"Y'all git comfy. I be right back," Gregory announced and flipped on the stereo as he went, most likely, to slip into something more comfortable. The Bee Gees' "How Deep is Your Love" murmured softly over the speakers hidden somewhere behind a stuffed raccoon holding a pack of Skittles.

Ronnie knew he couldn't go through with *Phase Three*. This knowledge was solidified as he observed the eyes staring back at him — lots of them — glued into the bodies of other taxidermied animals. A bear, screech owl, moose head and, positioned purposefully beside the pool, a Burmese Python eating a mouse — and a jar of Vaseline.

No. Way.

"D'ya want trunks or d'ya go skinny?" asked Gregory. He held a pair of neon green Speedos – just like the ones that now enveloped his own manhood.

"Uh, Greg? I think I may have given you the wrong impression. I'm not gay. I thought we were going to play some pool."

"Gay?" Gregory laughed. "Man, I ain't no gay! But yeah, that's the pool there."

Ronnie's mind mercifully blacked out what happened next. Thankfully, he had no idea what transpired in the moments it took from Gregory's denouncement of his homosexuality to the point where he found himself in the pool beside him.

A cigar was clenched haplessly between Gregory's lips. Ronnie cracked another beer and sipped it down through a chuckle. Gregory's punchline involved a female penguin whose last line was:

'Oh, that's just a little ice cream.'

"You know, this is a cool idea," Ronnie complimented.

"Who needs a Jacuzzi?" said Gregory and reached over for a hairdryer, which was connected to a vacuum hose, and turned it on. Bubbles began to blow into the pool.

Ronnie eased back against the plastic. It squeaked like soap. "Just wish my wife was here," he said. Initiating *Phase Three...*

Gregory's cigar glowed orange. "Yeah. A little three way, uh?"

"Don't be disgusting," Ronnie said.

"I just mean, I wish my lady was here, too," Gregory replied with a shrug.

Phase Three in three... two.... one.

"So, you see Oprah much around here?"

Gregory adjusted his Speedos making Ronnie very, very grateful to the mass of bubbles in the water. They obscured everything. "My family's owned this land for years. She happened to buy out a few of the neighbors farms some years back. Guess she needs land for her dogs."

"Dogs?"

Gregory let out a belch and reached for another beer. "Got about a dozen. I know the vet, Charlie. He's the one what gave me those," he gestured to the taxidermy critters. "He's the one who got me into Oprah, too. Charlie's going there tomorrow to give the dogs checkups."

Ronnie pondered the possibilities. He had no idea what the possibilities were, but that's what pondering was for.

"Hey, you like movies?" asked Gregory, not waiting for an answer. He grabbed the remote and clicked on his television – an old school tube type. He pushed *play*. An even older school VHS tape whirred inside the machine. Tonight's selection – *Debbie Does Everybody*.

And, Debbie wasted no time. Fade In on her and three other partners, already partaking in fleshy interests as a Casio keyboard provided the soundtrack.

"Uh... Greg?"

"Pass me a beer," Gregory requested, arm outstretched and palm waiting. Ronnie placed another Budweiser in his hand. Anything but the obvious to keep it busy.

"You know the worst thing about oral sex?" Gregory wanted to know.

Ronnie swallowed over a sudden lump in his throat. "What's that?"

"The view," he snickered and adjusted himself. He leaned forward and pointed to his back. There was a carpet of hair on it.

"Buddy, my back itches," he said. "Do me a favor and scratch it, will ya?"

Ronnie hesitated. Anyone would. Slowly, ever so slowly, he reached out his hand to the place between the hairs and the pimple at which Gregory pointed.

"Mmmm. Yeah. Mmmm, oh yeah.."

"Excuse me!" Ronnie tried not to shout, but it wasn't possible. "Need the bathroom."

"Right down the hall. At the end," Greg gestured.

Ronnie clamored out of the pool and sloshed his way out of the living room.

The snow fell to about half a foot. It was dark out here in the country, and cold, and wet, but Ronnie figured he could survive. He'd seen a couple episodes of *Survivorman*. How hard could it be?

Pretty hard, as it turned out. And,

Survivorman wasn't being hounded by a crazy not-gay hillbilly.

"Ronnie?" Gregory called through the darkness. "Hey, buddy, where'd ya go?"

Ronnie picked up the pace or tried to. His pair of donated cowboy boots weren't really made for trudging at speed through a snow pack, and one of the heels felt wobbly. He pressed on until he suddenly couldn't. A dull pain latched on to his ankle, as if he'd been bitten by a toothless bear or, more to the point, an old bear trap. Ronnie thumped on his ass and grabbed at his leg. He couldn't help it and let out an anguished cry.

"I'm coming, buddy!" Gregory yelled. He hadn't taken the time to change clothes and was still in his neon green Speedos. He did have the foresight to bring along a shotgun and a flashlight, though. He shined it through the woods and landed on Ronnie, struggling against a pair of rusty, iron jaws. "Hold on, buddy! I'll get you loose!"

Gregory dropped to his knees beside his new friend and began to pry the trap apart. Leverage was key here, and his butt wiggled right in Ronnie's face.

It can't get any worse. It can't possibly get any worse, Ronnie thought, then realized he'd just broken one of the most important karmatic laws in the universe. Indeed, it could get worse, because his nose was mere inches from Gregory's Speedo covered ass crack.

"Now yer talkin'," smiled Gregory. "But lemme get this here trap off first. Buddy."

Ronnie grimaced.

People crowded Legends like a meat market. Butter sat at the bar, not interested in the gyrating and sweating bodies that crushed themselves together on the dance floor, but rather something, or someone, else. Henry the barkeep poured him a rum and pointed out Shenique at the far end of the floor.

Butter tossed back his drink and made his way toward her.

Shenique eyed the newest Don Juan slinking through the dance floor and directly toward her — like a shark on dry land. He stopped in front of her, grinning toothy.

"You're blocking my view," said Shenique.

"Oh. Sorry," Butter moved a little to the side.

"You're still blocking my view. Try over there," Shenique pointed to the far end of the bar, hoping the guy would get the hint. She tried looking over his shoulder, trying to locate Denise because there was safety in numbers, but the guy was as big as Mount Everest.

"I'm Butter," Butter said.

Shenique raised her brow. "I'm Chiffon," she replied.

A deep laugh rumbled in Butter's throat. "That's funny," he said.

"No, it's corny. Oh, and look. It's Parkay," Shenique indicated Denise, taking longer than necessary to dance her way toward her.

"So, can we talk?" Butter asked.

"Sorry. I'm watching my cholesterol."

"Just give me a chance." Butter smiled, but Shenique in no way returned the sentiment.

Shenique knew there was only one way out of this. Denise shimmied her way to her side, in rhythm with Bob Marley and his Wailers, and was about to announce two cute business professionals who wanted to buy them drinks, when Shenique suddenly grabbed her, and planted a passionate kiss on her lips.

Butter just stood there, undeterred. "I'm not trying to get with your ass. I said I want to talk to you," he said, taking her arm.

Shenique snatched her Stun Gun from her purse and jolted her accoster with 100,000 volts.

Butter fell in spasms — a fish flapping out of water on the dance floor.

The dance floor stops and stares until, "Go Butter! ... Go Butter! ... Go Butter! " Shenique starts hyping him.

The rest of the dancehall joins along, "Go Butter! Go Butter!"

* * *

The queue in front of the Harpo Studios was packed, as usual. What was not usual was the amount of people dressed in blue pants suits, red blouses, red pumps, floppy white '70s hats and fake Gucci shades.

Bud pulled at his chin, disgusted with the human race. His eyes then lit on the lady in the wheelchair — Oprah's most devout zealot. His disgust level increased. Even she was attempting to assume the persona of the elusive Jane Doe Oprah saved at the Women's Conference. She wheeled up to him, her own suite and hate dangerously close to getting stuck in her wheels, which she had intrepidly modified to snow tires.

"Tell Oprah I've come out of hiding," she said, proudly.

"The woman they're looking for could walk." Bud crossed his arms in front of his chest.

"I could, too, before I fell out of that damn ambulance."

Bud rolled his eyes. "Nope. That happened just a couple of nights ago."

Wheelchair Lady curled her finger, indicating for Bud to come closer. He did. Better to sometimes humor the fanatic than to outright refuse. They were like ticking time bombs.

"C'mon, honey. Ain't nobody gonna know the difference." She put her face closer to his ear. "And, if there's a reward, I'll split it with ya."

"No, thanks," Bud said and took the handles of her wheelchair. Time to roll this one to the back of the line.

Wheelchair Lady would have none of it. She grabbed the brake, spun her chair like a gold medal Special Olympian, and slammed the footrest into Bud's shin. He doubled over, right in front of her. She grabbed his crotch with one hand and deftly flicked out a switchblade with the other, holding it dangerously close to Bud's man parts.

"Listen, honey," she said. "I may be in a wheelchair, but nobody pushes me around." With that, she released him. It was the season for mercy, after all. "Take your picture with the Wheelchair Lady! As seen on Oprah!" she announced to the crowd.

iPhones immediately raised, like lighters at a concert.

Ronnie began to rouse from a fitful sleep. He'd been dreaming of Beverly and himself at the Willis Tower. They were standing on the Plexiglas platform looking down at the ant-sized pedestrians below, when the Plexiglas suddenly disappeared. They fell, slowly. Denise fell with them, handing Beverly a business card from her law firm and telling her they definitely had a wrongful death case.

Right before impact, he awoke.

He was face to face with a black bear.

He screamed and pushed the bear off him. For a bear, it was pretty harmless. Being a rug and all.

Ronnie tried to get up, but it felt like he was trying to gain solid traction on a rolling sea. Which, in essence, he was. Gregory's waterbed mattress sloshed fore and aft.

"Good morning," Gregory sang. He set a breakfast tray on the nightstand. "I made you blueberry panycakes. Ya like blueberries?" he asked, removing Ronnie's bearskin cover. It was only then Ronnie realized he was tied to the bed… with Confederate flags. "Let me get that, buddy. I ain't want ya runnin' out and getting hurt again."

Gregory untied him and folded the flags carefully.

"What about my feet?" Ronnie asked through the lump in his throat. The lump that seemed to be becoming a permanent part of his anatomy.

"Yer feet ain't tied," Gregory replied, as if it should have been obvious.

Ronnie looked down and found that his foot

was encased in a concrete block.

Gregory crossed the room and turned on the television. He adjusted the rabbit ears.

Dana's face came through crystal clear — her and her Bartlesby Funds commercial. "At Bartlesby Funds, we don't weigh down your assets with poor performers. We dump them fast. It's what grew us from number three to number one. And we're still getting better all the time," she finished with a flourishing smile.

"I ain't have no plaster," Gregory explained. "So I used concrete. Figured it work just as good. Ain't too keen on going out in da snow."

Ronnie wiggled the toes of his encased foot. "How do you know it's broke?"

"Can't take no chances. Oh, hey! Look who's on."

Gregory fixed his attention to the television and gave it a solid pop. The horizontal hold cleared, just as the photograph of Ronnie – knocked unconscious by a hotel planter – disappeared from the screen.

"So, if you've seen her, call the number on your screen," Oprah instructed. "It could mean one hundred thousand dollars."

Ronnie's head began to spin. "Could you turn that off, please?"

"Are you serious? If it weren't for Ms. Winfrey, we'd a never met."

"Yeah. Ironic, isn't it?"

As if on cue, Oprah continued, "Have you ever felt trapped? If so, here's what you can do about it. Next. On Oprah."

Jazzy fusion. Funky snare beat. It was a

sound Ronnie was equating with Satan's theme, if
Satan had one.

"S'cuse me a sec, Ronnie," Gregory said and
left the room, subsequently leaving Ronnie and his
concrete block in Oprah's broadcasted presence. She
was reading from the back of John Gray's latest book.

"'Next time you're feeling trapped, look at
your life,'" read Oprah to her viewers. "'Evaluate
how you got there, figure out your options and devise
your best plan. Then put that plan into action.'"

Ronnie scowled. That's what he had been
doing and it landed him on a waterbed in a concrete
shoe. *What bullshit*.

Oprah smiled, put the book aside, and glowed
for the camera. "As Mister Gray teaches, each trap
you land in is set by your subconscious to help you
grow stronger."

"Yeah?" Ronnie said to Oprah's image. "How
many subconsciousness know how to pour concrete?"

"Who you talkin' to?" Gregory asked
suddenly appearing at the foot of the waterbed, with a
sledgehammer. "And, what was all that crazy you
was talkin' last night, about getting to Oprah?"

"I said something?" Ronnie asked, instantly
terrified. "Oprah is a saint, Gregory."

"That ain't what you said last night," Gregory
said, nonchalantly placing Ronnie's concrete foot on a
block of wood, like Nurse Annie Wilkes in *Misery*.

"Last night?" Ronnie's mind raced, searching
for some way to distract Gregory.

"After the Jack Daniels for the pain, you had a
lot to say 'bout her. None too nice."

Amnesia must have taken hold of Ronnie —
or an alcohol-induced black out or Post-Traumatic

Stress Disorder. He remembered nothing.
"Whiskey? Oh, that must be it! I was drunk," he
said, as he watched Gregory line up the hammer to
block like Tiger Woods lining up at the tee. "Wait!
Just wait!" Ronnie screamed.

"For what?" asked Gregory.

"Look, Greg. Friend. I have to get to Oprah,
and I looked you up because you said you lived next
to her. See, I'm all messed up, Greg. My whole life."

Gregory placed the business end of the
sledgehammer on the carpet and leaned against the
handle. He may as well listen to what his new friend
had to say. Even though it probably wouldn't change
anything. Friends don't use each other.

But, listen he did… to Ronnie's entire tale of
woe. It was like a bad country song. He'd lost his
love, his money, his dad, and got stoned — a lot. And
at the end, felt as if he were cursed. Ronnie said he
couldn't win, so he cheated. He did to others as they
had done to him.

Gregory sighed and raised the sledgehammer
like Sammy Sosa at the plate.

Ronnie's eyes went as wide as platters. After
all that, after this whole confession, Gregory was still
going full Annie Wilkes on him?

Gregory brought down the hammer with the
dexterity of a jeweler. It hit the concrete block at just
the right spot, at just the right angle, with just the
right amount of force.

It fell harmlessly away from Ronnie's foot.

"Y' never said if you liked blueberries,"
Gregory said.

As a matter of fact, Ronnie did like
blueberries. They'd taste even better, accompanied by

the general gratitude he felt for still being alive and two-footed.

Chapter Eight

The microwave in Beverly's hotel room beeped announcing that her Jimmy Dean Sausage Sandwiches were ready. Beverly shuffled across the tiled floor of the kitchenette and took them out. Little steamy piles of processed pork stared back at her.

Beverly dumped them in the trashcan. She glanced to the digital display clock — ten in the morning. She sighed and tied her hotel bathrobe tighter. As she stood there, wishing she were deep in thought, she realized she wasn't. She felt numb all over. She had nowhere to be. Sure, her brain in the throes of muscle memory reminded her that she was late for work. Beverly reminded her brain that she wasn't. The boxes packed with her belongings from the agency reminded them both of that fact.

Boxes of belongings. Bad sausage. Claustrophobic hotel room. Had it really gotten this bad?

It had.

Beverly sat on the edge of the bed just beside her office box. She opened the lid, aimlessly. On top, those darned pictures of her and Ronnie. She chewed the inside of her lip. Why had she brought them? Why did she keep bringing them? Everywhere she went, they followed her. Like a strip of toilet paper stuck on her shoe. It occurred to her, just then, that she knew where the pictures belonged. In the trash can, beside the bad sausage. It was a perfect juxtaposition.

She took the pictures and pushed the lid of the garbage open with her foot. Just as she was going to toss them, she paused, holding the picture of her estranged husband at Grant Park just above the receptacle. Yet, it wasn't Ronnie she was looking at. It was the landscape behind him.

Beverly remembered taking the picture. And remembered, as well, that her hotel room offered her the same view. She ran to the window and pulled the curtains apart.

The Park glistened with sunlit snow. Lake Michigan was green beyond it, a beautiful blanket beneath a bright azure sky. Beverly's fingers framed it in shot — the perfect shot. Without Ronnie, or any face for that matter, it was even better.

She ran to the desk and pulled out the Hilton complimentary note pad and pen. She wrote, furiously.

Business Plan – Beverly Bunn-Jones-Bunn-Jones-Mitchell-Bunn Advertising.

Beverly scratched out *Advertising*, and replaced it with *Photography*.

She tapped the pen against her teeth, smiled, and crossed out every last name except her own.

Beverly Bunn Photography.

Now that looked good.

Ronnie chewed the last of the blueberry panycakes. They were actually quite tasty. Gregory even sizzled up some pork links, too. Ronnie was about to compliment him on his culinary technique, but Gregory held up his finger. He was on the phone.

The other line picked up. "Happy Paws. This is Charlie, the vet for your pet," Charlie himself announced. His assistant called in sick today.

Ronnie could hear him. Gregory was a trifle deaf in one ear, so he had to crank the volume to ten.

"Charlie! Slipshank, here!"

Charlie's voice went from pleasant to paranoid in one shake of a dog's tail. "Listen to me, you blow-up-pool, porno-watching, taxidermy freak. I warned you to quit calling here or I'm calling the cops."

Gregory sopped up the last of the syrup with a pork link. "Sure, partner. Fine. Thanks for asking."

"What the hell is your problem?" Charlie's filtered voice growled.

"Actually, I need a favor."

"Are you out of your freakin' mind?"

Gregory smiled at Ronnie and winked. Ronnie wasn't going to return the wink, as it might imply something.

"A friend of mine needs to get a message to Oprah, Charlie. I figured since you're going there tonight –"

Ronnie could hear Charlie's teeth grinding as he responded.

"I'm hanging up, you nutcase. Do you hear me?"

"Much oblige. We'll call you tonight."

The click of Charlie making good on his last statement came through Gregory's phone. "Sure, we'll go bowling next week. Bring the wife and kids…. Hey, you, too, Charlie," Gregory put the phone back on the cradle and turned to Ronnie. "He says he'll help."

"He called you a freak and hung up," Ronnie said.

"You heard, uh?"

"Bullshitting doesn't win you true friends, Greg. Believe me, I know. It can even lose you a true love."

Gregory nodded as he contemplated just that. He could relate. "Y'know what? If you can wait a bit, I know how to help you."

Ronnie watched as Gregory crossed to the pantry and took a video tape from his extensive collection. A strange place to store videos, behind the Captain Crunch and Bisquick, but Ronnie assumed these were private tapes, and Gregory had issues.

Gregory plucked out the tape labeled "Charlie". It had a heart drawn on it with Sharpie. He tucked it underneath his shirt.

"Back it two shakes," he said.

Beverly was unemployed, and she'd never been busier. She'd ordered room service – no sausage, thank you – and finished the last of her blueberry pancakes. Thirty bucks for a couple of flapjacks was an extravagance, for certain, but one lives once. She wiped her hands together, chugged down another sip of coffee, and set back to work.

Her computer screen had seven windows open and running at once — a little NASA. There were flow charts, spread sheets, and Power Point presentations. An intricate draft of her future studio was drawn on the complimentary notepad.

Beverly opened an eighth window – this one labeled as Oprah's To Do's – and highlighted the last one. It was the only item not checked.

Make peace with those who have hurt you.

"Easier read than done," she said. Even so, she set the font to 18, clicked on bold, italic, and *underline*, selected all caps, and typed:

DON'T BE AFRAID

Beverly tucked a stray curl of hair behind her ear and studied her screen. Her bold-fonted advice was the last on the To Do list, and would be, by far, the most difficult — and interestingly enough, the most frightening.

Henry wiped the last spots of the shot glasses with his tank top. Every washrag was in the laundry, but he had a job to do. He held one up to the light, inspecting it through a squint, then squinted harder. The door opened, letting the harsh winter light inside. It was before business hours, though, so Henry couldn't think of why someone would be coming in at this time — someone either unusually desperate or drunk… or both.

It was neither. Denise came inside, wringing her hands. "Hi, Henry," she said, still hand wringing. She was nervous as hell. Denise harbored a secret crush on Henry (he reminded her so much of the sensual and sensitive Francisco). Being around him always made her jittery, in a good way. She cleared her throat, "Did I leave my purse?"

"Sexy Denise," smiled Henry, unknowingly sending Denise's insides spiraling about like a carnival ride. He reached under the bar and gave her her handbag. "All dat scuffin' last night, it got way from you," Henry said, pointing to the bag. "Your stuff's still dere?"

"I'm sure you've... I mean," Denise cleared her throat again and peeked inside her purse... everything present and accounted for. "It's got everything I need... everything I want... everything I brought, that is... thanks," she said and said no more because she knew she was rumbling off at the mouth like an idiot.

A quiet smile etched on Henry's face. He liked this one — for reals. "No problems. But, say, d'ya know what dat was all about last night?" Henry started shaking, imitating being electrocuted by an invisible stun gun.

"Oh, that," Denise said, remembering Butter floundering on the floor, a victim to Shenique's weapon of choice. "The guy wanted to know about Ronnie. He was a bit short on manners, and well... you know Shenique."

"Ah. Dey worked it out, though."

"They did? Huh. I wouldn't know. I left without her. Okay. Well. Thanks again. Henry," she managed and turned to leave. She wished she could work it out. Something, anything out. She didn't want to end up like stupid Rosa from the book. Turning her back on the amazing, handsome, gentle Francisco because the handmaiden decided to become a merchant marine. Just weird. And stupid. Pathetic, like herself. And pathetic, she no longer wanted to be. "Henry?"

"Yah?"

Denise sucked in a huge breath. "Are you busy tonight because there's this Christmas party I've been invited to and I hate to go alone and I'd really love to go with you but I guess you're working, right?

Okay, sorry. Bye!" She opened the door, wishing for a great big hole to open up outside the door and swallow her.

There was no hole, only her Honda waiting loyally at the curb. She fumbled with the key, never being able to tell where the unlock button was, *ever*. She was so *dumb*.

"Denise!" Henry yelled behind her, instantly wrapping his bare arms around himself as he neglected to throw a coat over his tank top. "It's my night off!" he shouted.

Denise slid into her car. "Yeah, I wasn't thinking. Thanks again!" She turned the ignition, and revved the motor.

"But I said I'm off tonight! I'd love to go!"

The Honda pulled away from the curb, its tires losing traction on the snow and ice. If Denise hadn't been cranking the engine so high, she may have heard Henry. But, alas, she did not. She didn't even have the courage to look in the rear view mirror. Which turned out to be a good thing, as Henry's slush-covered figure would have been the image she saw.

"Way to go Denise," Denise criticized herself. "Open mouth, insert foot."

She hated being lame. Denise punched the power knob on her stereo. Ella Fitzgerald's buttery vocals began to croon.

"Oh the weather outside is frightful, but the fire is so delightful, and since we've no place to go..."

Denise grunted. No place to go. Just like her. Stupid Christmas songs.

Ronnie hummed along with the stereo as he

placed the last dish in the washer.

"Oh the fire's slowly dyin', but, my dear, we're still good-byein'..."

"Hello!" Gregory sang from the front entry way. He shook snow off his coat and gestured for his companion to come inside. Charlie left his coat and satchel on, snow and all. He pushed up his rim-framed glasses and pursed his lips together at the sight of the inflatable pool and Ronnie, as he took off an apron that suggested one to *Kiss The Cook!* "What'd I tell you? Ron Mitchell, Charles Blanks – Mister Happy Paws himself."

Ronnie hung his apron and extended his hand to Charlie. Charlie shook it. Good boy.

"Charlie's gonna let you do his check up for him," Gregory gushed. He was positively giddy.

"But, I don't know anything about dogs," Ronnie said.

"There's nothing wrong with them," Charlie returned, not attempting to hide his personal disgust. "She just has them checked every three months. Go look at them, tell her they're fine, then say what's on your mind."

"I can't just go with you?"

"The guards will make you wait at the gate. No need for two vets. They'll call to verify I sent you. I'll just call in sick as it were."

Gregory shuddered in delight. He loved it when Charlie sounded all sophisticated and Bostonian.

Charlie opened his satchel, the snow falling to the bare spot in the rug, and produced a Happy Paws ball cap and jacket. Ronnie tried them on. A little snug, but they'd do.

"Thanks," Ronnie said. He looked at the gleaming Gregory, then back to Charlie. Charlie looked as if he'd been sucking on a particularly sour lemon. Ronnie gestured between the two men. "You two are cool after all?"

Gregory took the Charlie VHS tape from his coat and nodded.

"Yeah." Charlie stated flatly.

"You was just playin' round, right Charlie?" Gregory gave a sly look to Ronnie. "We used to play around all the time."

Charlie let out a quiet, forced chuckle. The kind one would have on the way to the gallows.

Later that day, the Happy Paws Honda CRV sat idling in front of Oprah's guardhouse. Ronnie drummed his fingers against the wheel, attempting to look casual. It was a nice ride for dogs. Leather interior, onboard GPS, and seat warmers. Even the little kennels in the back were wired for heat and comfort.

A heavy duty security guard, quite possibly from the same gene pool as Bud the Bodyguard, held the guard shack phone to his ear. "Well, okay, Blanks. Get well soon," he said, replaced the phone, and buzzed the CRV through the gates.

Charlie ended his call and stared at Gregory sitting across from him in the pool, smiling.

Gregory clicked on the hair dryer.

Ronnie turned the CRV's seat warmers to high

and settled his buns into the leather as he wound his way through Oprah's massive estate. *Winter Wonderland* played through the speakers, a perfect accentuation to the property he drove through. Busy pines covered in show dotted the lawn. Massive branches on huge oak trees created a natural canopy above the road. A magnificent French country manor home, Oprah's main house was decorated with miles of red, green, and gold lights. Behind it, also adorned in a mass of holiday wattage, was a barn. Not just any barn, though. This one was as long as a city block and had its own heliport complete with helicopter.

The CRV stopped in front of the barn. Ronnie got out and made his way inside.

The luckiest, and perhaps the largest, pack of golden retrievers on the planet watched *Lassie* on a giant flat screen. Each of them turned their perfectly groomed, golden heads as Ronnie entered. The leader of the luckiest pack, a retriever with a spot of black, like a little goatee underneath his chin, got up to investigate their visitor. His tag identified him as Samson, which Ronnie took note of as the dog sniffed his hand then gave him a welcome lick.

"Hey, Samson," Ronnie said. "You look healthy to me."

Samson sat and wagged his tail.

The rear doorbell of the manor house chimed pleasantly. A manor house security guard, Stanley, sipped down the last of his hot cocoa and opened the door. Ronnie stood on the other side, smiling, and holding a Happy Paws manila envelope.

"Hi," Ronnie began. He was half-hoping

Oprah would have greeted him at the door. Then the fun would really have begun. "Just want to give Ms… uh… Winfrey, the, uh…. Report on her dogs."

"Oh, you can leave it with me," Stanley offered, holding out his hand for the envelope. His palm was as big as a dinner plate. It seemed that no male under Oprah's employ was less than six foot tall or under two hundred and twenty pounds.

"What? Oh, um… no, that won't work," Ronnie stammered.

"Why not?"

"Because, I mean… uh… there's a, a problem." That sounded plausible to Ronnie. Like Indiana Jones, he was making this up as he went along.

"Is it serious?" Stanley asked. He sure hoped not. He liked those dogs.

"Yes, I'm afraid. Very. Very, urgent. Hurry," Ronnie exclaimed and ran back to the CRV. Stanley took the walkie-talkie from his belt. Ms. Winfrey must be informed immediately.

Inside the CRV, the seats still warm, Ronnie fished out a medical case. He searched through it, frantically, until he found a bottle of Mercurochrome. That should do the trick. Ronnie put the transmission in drive and floored it.

The luckiest dogs on the planet each sat obediently, calmly, tongues dropping out of their mouths in their constant state of canine bliss as the man dabbed a little bit of the red fluid on their paws.

They looked like dog freckles.

The barn door swung open, revealing Stanley and a very, very upset Oprah.

"Stay back!" Ronnie instructed then pointed at Stanley. "Have you been in contact with the dogs?"

"No, I –"

"Then stay outside!"

Stanley did as he was told. Oprah came in, every single tail wagging in absolute primal delight as she did so.

"What is it?" Oprah asked, nervously.

Ronnie took Samson's paw, and showed it to her. "Have you seen this before?" he asked, pretty sure he was coming across as professional.

"Oh, God, no. I haven't..." Samson licked her face. "What is that?"

"It looks like early stages of… paw and mouth. Yes. We've got to get them to the clinic. They may all be infected."

Oprah looked up at him, doubtful. All the dogs looked perfectly healthy to her. "You're kidding."

"Paw and mouth is potentially fatal, and if one has it, they all have it. There's no time to waste here."

"But they look fine."

Ronnie was beginning to sweat. She wasn't cooperating and his veterinary knowledge was slim — alright, non-existent, but still. He'd have to turn this up a notch. Panic was good.

"You might be infected, too. This is what killed my dog. My God. I don't want to see that again. It's horrible. Horrible! The fur falls out. Then their lips crack."

Samson yawned, and stretched out in front of

Oprah's feet.

"Then..." Ronnie searched his brain for more. "Then the farts. The farts are the worst. You've never smelled such vile!"

Stanley peeked his head inside. The Happy Paws guy was yelling about flatulence… urgently, too. "Is it like rotten eggs?" he asked.

"Stay back!" Ronnie held up his hands. "So much worse than eggs! So much worse! You'd need an army of Martha Stewarts hyped up on crack to clean that smell out of your house!"

Oprah paused. The guy sounded sincere and worried, but he was just an assistant. He could have misdiagnosed. But, as she saw the dozens of hopeful, loving, big brown eyes staring back at her, she determined she could not take a chance.

"Okay, guys," she said to the dogs. "Come!"

The luckiest and largest pack on the planet instantly obeyed. Like a stampede of yellow fur and fluff, they eagerly followed Oprah out to the CRV.

Moments later, the Happy Paws CRV was loaded stem to stern with literal happy paws — a dozen of them, happily drooling, wagging, and licking.

Oprah clutched the dashboard as Charlie's assistant drove the truck across her property like Mario Andretti. Stanley followed behind, as he had been ordered not to come into close contact with the animals. His large black Durango rode the Happy Paws bumper like a presidential escort.

"What about the other people who've been in contact with them?" she asked as Samson licked her face. "My staff, friends, family —"

Ronnie blew through the gates and kept it floored.

Well, no better time than the present, he thought.

"There's nothing wrong with your dogs."

"What?"

"I need to talk to you, and the guard wasn't going to let me see you."

Oprah swallowed nervously. She was being kidnapped. But she had read enough self-help books to know what to do in this sort of situation. John Gray had a great one on Stockholm Syndrome, and Oprah knew that it was better not to fuel the fire but diffuse it with calm rationality. Besides, the idiot nabbed her along with a dozen loyal, very possessive, very *protective* animals.

"What would you like to talk about?" she asked, looking at him with the pre-prescribed rational calm. It was strange, though, as the kidnapper looked a little familiar.

"What I'm not getting about life," Ronnie said, gripping the steering wheel a little tighter. There was an icy patch in the road coming up and traffic. From his pocket, his cell phone chimed that he had a new message.

It hit Oprah like a mallet. This was the guy from her studio, the one who brought the contraband phone inside. "You!"

"I tried to reach you so many ways," he looked at her, the brim of his Happy Paws hat pulled down just enough to cast a sinister shadow over his face. "I finally get to talk to you," he grinned. Looking even more sinister.

Oprah would employ hostage tactic number eleven, according to Gray, and quietly put her hand on the handle. She wished herself luck, as John Gray never stepped foot out of Illinois, and therefore, his advice to potential terrorist victims was most likely fictional.

The traffic ahead slowed. Ronnie eased his foot off the accelerator. Oprah opened the door and jumped from the truck.

"Hey!" Ronnie shouted, looking back, seeing Oprah do a ninja-roll on the snow and then leap to her feet. Stanley slammed to a stop beside her. She climbed inside his black Durango.

He was about to give chase, when suddenly, the CRV stopped, signaled, and pulled over to the curb.

"Are you okay?" Ronnie asked. And was met by gunfire in return.

He ducked, covered his head, and ran back to the CRV.

"Freeze!" Stanley yelled, leaning out the window and leveling his gun. He'd *always* wanted to do this!

Oprah grabbed Stanley's arm. "Don't shoot! You might hit the dogs!"

The Happy Paws CRV screeched away from the curb.

Stanley put the Durango back into drive and floored it. The Hemi made little work of catching up to Ronnie and was breathing down his tailpipe.

At 70 miles per hour, the Happy Paws CRV struggled to stay ahead of the much larger and more powerful pursuer.

The trees on Oprah's property bowed against the force of a sudden, gale-force wind. Snow blew from the branches creating a stand-alone hurricane.

The helicopter lifted from the pad.

Police Captain Jones wiped the remains of a blueberry fritter off his chin and reached for another. He and his new partner, rookie officer Cliff, had met up with another unit and were in the midst of enjoying a much-deserved donut break – yes, yes, they knew the stereotypical implications – when Captain Jones' radio crackled to life.

"Attention all units. I-80 west, ten thirty-one in progress. Possible ten ninety-six. White Honda CRV, license Paul, Alfa, Whiskey, Sierra, Romeo, Uniform, Sierra."

Jones selected an apple turnover. "Ten thirty-one is a crime in progress," he said to Cliff. "What's a ten ninety-six?"

Cliff flipped his notepad open and scanned it. "Uh... mental patient."

"Ten four," Jones said, taking his fritter to go.

"Units be advised," the radio crackled again. "Ten thirty-one involves Oprah Winfrey."

Jones dropped the fritter and ran outside. Followed by the rest of those sworn to serve and protect.

Samson took it upon himself to procure the shotgun position. He loved car rides. He had a little trouble keeping his balance, as the man driving kept swerving and dodging their way down the highway. He licked his lips, panted, and stared at Ronnie.

"What?" Ronnie asked, careening around an Oldsmobile with a broken tail light.

Samson woofed.

"What do you expect me to do, huh? They were shooting at me! She thinks I'm nuts!"

Samson wagged his tail.

Chapter Nine

Beverly's bags were packed and ready to go. This would be her last night in the hotel. On the bed, a tasteful black dress was laid out and ready, just beside the party invitation from Ted and Linda Mitchell.

The bathroom door popped open and Beverly emerged in a cloud of steam, her natural curls standing straight up from the leave in conditioner, singing "I'm Mister Heatmiser. I'm Mister Sun. I'm Mister Green Christmas. I'm Mister hundred and one!" *The Year Without a Santa Claus* played on the TV behind her. "Whatever I touch, starts to melt in my clutch," Beverly sang as she sat at the vanity. "I'm too much." She took the towel from her body and looked at her reflection. She didn't feel like she was Too Much — maybe all that, minus the bag of chips. She was a tad unsettled, being an hour or so away from visiting her estranged in-laws, but it was a column on hers and Oprah's to-do list, and she was psyching herself up to go through with it.

She scanned the vanity, looking for her hairbrush. It would take her a while to twist her coif away from the Heatmiser style she was celebrating. Realizing she'd left it in on the bathroom counter, she got up to retrieve it. Thereby missing the Breaking News. Channel Four cut away from Mister Heatmiser to report a high-speed chase on I-80.

The network chopper kept its regulated FAA-ordained distance as it flew above the highway. The camera man held the white CRV, the Dodge Durango and a line of police cars in shot. There was an intersection up ahead, anyway, and those were always good for drama. He zoomed in as four additional squad cars converged at Fifth and Meadow. The CRV accelerated, fishtailing as it made the light.

The squad cars weren't so fortunate. For reasons that the police department would later equate to poor tire pressure, the latest black and whites to join the fray slammed into each other, leaving only Captain Jones and Officer Cliffs' vehicle in the chase.

The Durango maneuvered around the pile up and followed along now behind the officer's car. Then, screw this I'm Oprah Winfrey, it pulled to a stop beside a vacant lot. Dust, dirt and a flurry of fresh powder lofted from the ground and into the sky like a tornado.

Oprah's private helicopter touched down. Sure, that was breaking every single air space regulation the government had ever dreamed of, but this was an emergency, and Oprah was Oprah. She ran out of the Durango and to the helicopter.

It lifted into the sky.

Rookie officer Cliff looked on at Captain Jones as he pressed the button on the radio mike. Cliff felt as though he was going to wet himself. This was just like *Adam-12* and *Starsky and Hutch*, and Cliff felt a little tinge of embarrassed for his Netflix binge-watching of old, hokey police shows. But,

Captain Jones recommended them.

"Illinois Patrol, please be advised we are tracking a ten ninety six into your jurisdiction. Request back up," Jones said.

The radio replied, "Attention all available units. Indiana Patrol requests back up on 10-96 at I-80 border. Copy?"

Illinois Patrol Dispatch confirmed.

Chestnuts roasted on an open fire, literally. It was one of those personal, intimate touches Freda insisted on for her and Ted's annual holiday get-together. They were a pain in the ass and no one ever ate them, but Freda had seen a piece on the Oprah Winfrey Christmas Cheer Special a few years ago and had been doing it ever since.

Freda tended to the copper pan above the fireplace – the Duraflame log not quite up to the task of roasting but it was the thought that counted – and shook the nuts about like Jiffy Pop.

Ted wound his way through his party guests, sipping on fat-free egg nog on his way to the door. He thought he heard the bell ring. He glanced over to Freda bent over the fire and the nuts. Ted grinned – the woman had a fine, fine backside – and opened the door.

"Hi, who are you?" he asked.

Denise waved, bashfully. "I'm Beverly's friend, Denise, and this… this is..." she pointed even more bashfully to Henry, who was holding a hostess-gift bottle of Appleton Estate. "Henry."

"Oh, hey. Welcome. Enjoy yourself," Ted said and gestured for them to come inside.

Henry handed off the Appleton. "Good stuff, mon," he said and followed Denise to the buffet.

Samson and the rest of the luckiest pack of golden retrievers munched happily on Milkbones, extra meaty flavor. Ronnie found them in the center console and was munching on one himself, as it was helping to sooth his nerves. He was still in the middle of a police pursuit, maneuvering his way down the highway, through the traffic, making sure to use his turn signals and keeping the recommended Two Mississippi Count between him and the cars in front. He didn't need any extra charges filed against him. Because once he got to the Stony Island off-ramp, the one that would lead eventually to Champion Court, all bets were off.

Ronnie glanced in the rear view, checked his teeth, and the patrol car careening behind him. He spat out a little chunk of dog biscuit and killed the lights in the CRV. Ronnie's plan was a simple one – he would be stealthy, a clandestine operative in a luxury urban vehicle. The sprawling area where his brother lived was literally crisscrossed with dark, quiet streets. One quick left on Elm and a clever-ass double back on Pine Street, and Ronnie put a substantial distance between him and the patrol car.

Shenique smoothed the front pleats of her dress – a hot little holiday number in shimmering red and green. Butter thought she looked like a sexy Christmas ornament. He could barely take his hands off her, even here, on the front stoop of a quaint house on Champion Court. Butter moved in to kiss her, oh-so-smoothly as was his nickname's manifesto, and was met with a quick jolt from her Panther Stun Gun. His thigh tingled.

"What a woman," Butter grinned.

"You behave inside," Shenique said. "If Ronnie's there, wait to get him outside. I don't want to spoil the party."

Butter crossed his heart. "Promise."

"I can't wait for that scrub to get his."

Ted opened the door and let them inside. He took a moment to regard Shenique's escort. Like a giant brick wall with features and a dinner jacket. So intrigued was Ted, he did not notice the white CRV with a big dog paw emblem zooming toward the house.

The helicopter belonged to Oprah hovered far, far above Champion Court, affording its passengers a birds' eye view of the Happy Paws transport pulling into a driveway.

The driver's door of the Happy Paws truck – the one with the smiling cartoon dog with a thermometer in its mouth – flew open. Ronnie jumped out and ran to the back of the house. It was dark around the back of the house, unfortunately, and Ronnie slammed into all three trash, recyclable, and garden-trimming containers in succession.

Misty slunk out from the backyard, perturbed by the latest noise. The house was full of noise, which is why she left, seeking sound asylum in the yard. It worked for a while but not long enough. The garbage containers rolling around the ground were five levels of irritating, and Misty was irritated to begin with. She slinked down the driveway, tail puffed with annoyance.

Every pair of Golden Retriever eyes locked on the cat. *Cat cat cat cat cat....*

The hood of the CRV was warm... deliciously warm. Misty jumped up on it and curled herself into a fluffy, contented ball.

Ronnie snuck through the back door of the kitchen, still attempting to employ his ninja tactics to remain unseen. It didn't work at all. Take the garbage cans, for example. However, Ted and Freda's party guests were in escalating stages of intoxications, so the guy wearing the Happy Paws baseball cap was really not a thing.

Now that Ronnie was here, he needed to get his head together and try and formulate a plan. His making-it-up-as-he-went had worked up to this point, but now, he needed an organized program. So much to do, so little time to do it. He could hear hovering helicopter blades and knew he had only moments until the police would find the glaring white SUV in his brother's driveway. He'd tiptoe his way up the stairs, think things through calmly, rationally, and quickly.

Butter took a snifter of Appleton rum from his lips, watching as a guy in a khaki shirt and ball cap snuck up the stairs. Interestingly enough, the khaki guy looked a hell of a lot like Ronnie Mitchell.

Butter grinned. Maybe this was his Christmas present. He'd been a moderately good boy this year.

Ronnie paced in front of Freda's full length mirror, running his hands over his hair in an effort to coax his next move from his brain.   All he could think about, and all he could hear were his pacing footsteps making the floor boards creak. The stairs were creaking, too. Someone big was on their way up.

Samson was positively drooling with excitement, staring at the cat on the hood of the CRV. He placed his paw on the Unlock icon of his door, took the handle in his teeth, and pulled inwards. Samson and his fuzzy colleagues piled out. Misty hissed, arched her back, and then took off like a bullet toward the house.

And her pet door.

That was in the kitchen.

The pet door looked like a big rubber party favor – flap, flap, flapping as an unending stream of uber-excited Golden Retrievers streamed through it… a raging river of fur, tongues, and absolute happy. Half of the pack slid to a stop in the kitchen, jumping up on tables and counters that were filled with appetizers, cream puffs, and a cold cut platter. The others blasted across the linoleum on their fully charged way into the living room.

Tables upended. Glasses dropped, wine and egg nog spilled onto the carpet and would never completely come out. Freda and her plate of roasted chestnuts were knocked to the floor, plowed into by Samson and his eager cohorts.   They bounded up the stairs.

Beverly was going to ring the doorbell, but the insanity she was hearing from inside gave her reason to pause. Had the party gotten this out of hand? Ted and Freda seemed like such classy people, they'd never throw what sounded like a frat party-times-ten. Then she heard sirens approaching and realized there was a helicopter, too, right above the house.

What the f- - -?

"C'mon, Butter," Ronnie implored. "Why not just let this slide?"

"I might have, if you hadn't run – played me for a punk."

Butter pushed his massive, caveman chest against Ronnie's. Time for this cowardly little weasel to pay the piper.

"That wasn't a good move, eh?" Ronnie stated the obvious. Butter was driving him back to the wall, like a snowplow. "You know, it doesn't matter. It happened. It's in the past. Things didn't work as planned, but that's okay. I just have to deal with it."

"What the hell are you talking about?"

"I can pay you, just not yet."

"But time's up, dog," Butter shoved Ronnie closer to the wall. He'd smoosh him like a bug.

"I just realized something," Ronnie said through what appeared to be a very badly timed smile. This climactic stage in his life was like the dramatic conclusion to a final act. It could end no other way, and Ronnie, for one, was glad it was over. "I'm going to be alright," he announced in a revelatory fashion.

"That's what you think," Butter said and went in for the final, fatal crush.

Just as Misty rocketed through Butter's legs and leapt into Ronnie's arms.

Samson and his colleagues were next – pushing Butter over as if he were nothing more than a bowling pin. Butter flailed for balance, but he was already at terminal velocity. His head smashed against the wall, knocking him out.

Misty clawed into Ronnie's shoulder, trying to climb him as if he were a tree. Samson and the other dogs barked, barked, barked relentlessly, wanting a piece of that feline.

"Samson! Hush!" Ronnie commanded.

Samson whined and sat as did the others. Misty settled in the crook of Ronnie's arm, a low grumble resonating from her throat.

Ronnie stroked her head, and her grumble began to dissipate. Ronnie took a huge breath, stepped over Butter and headed for *Phase Four*.

Catastrophe. Disaster. Complete cataclysm.

Freda wept over her chestnuts. Ted put his hand on her back to comfort her, but she smacked it away. Her holiday party was completely ruined. She watched through red-rimmed eyes as her invited guests picked themselves up off the floor, and food splatter from their clothes. The only ones who didn't seem any worse for wear were Denise and Henry. They were entranced with each other.

Linda, who had spent the entire time in the bathroom because lactose-intolerance and egg nog don't mix, stepped over broken plates and punch bowls as she made her way toward Freda. Freda looked as if she could really, really use some support. Linda knew how she felt about her chestnuts.

Ronnie stepped from the last stair with Misty in his arms and the pack of canines obediently behind. He surveyed the calamity before him. The calamity that he knew he caused.

Freda looked up from her fallen nuts. Her eyes locked on him.

"You!" Freda screamed. "I knew it! I'm going to kill you!" She picked herself up – screw the chestnuts – and was going to attack her idiot, party-killing brother-in-law, but Linda held her back.

The front door opened just a crack. Beverly peeked inside.

Ronnie continued to pet Misty's head. He and the cat were surrounded by Samson and the other dogs. Ronnie looked squarely at Freda. "I'm sorry," he said.

"Just leave, Ronnie," Freda spat. "Get out!"

Ted chimed in unexpectedly. "No, Ronnie. Wait," he said and took a check from his pocket. "I've been looking for you. I wanted to give you this." He held up a cashier's check in the amount of five thousand dollars.

Freda's eyes popped from their sockets. "You're giving him money? Are you out of your mind?"

"Thanks, Ted. But, just give it to the guy upstairs, okay?"

Ted's hand dropped. What guy upstairs?

"I'm not going to tell you again, Ronnie," warned Freda, hotly. "Get out of here!"

"You can't throw Ronnie out of his house, Freda," Ted said. He was full of the unexpected this evening.

Ronnie shook his head. "Ted, it's cool. I'll go."

"You own this house free and clear," Ted turned to Freda. "The money we pay goes into a trust fund Ronnie set up for Mamma. To make it look like dad left her provided for."

"What?" Freda stammered.

Ted shrugged. "I couldn't get financed, baby. We make payments for twenty years, or until Mamma dies, then the house is ours. Ronnie didn't want you to know because he thought you might try to kill Mom."

Freda's eyes narrowed. It was an interesting thought.

"Guys, I'm going, okay?" Ronnie said, sheepishly. He turned to the front door and came face to face with Beverly. Her hair was coifed naturally in twists and her features were lit in etheric lights of red and blue. Oprah's landing helicopter and the patrol cars surrounding the house certainly did cast her in an extraordinary air.

Oprah ran from the helicopter and frantically pointed at Ronnie. "That's him!"

"Drop the cat and come away from the house!" Captain Jones ordered from the squad car megaphone as Rookie officer Cliff kept his hand on his holster, just like Sergeant Friday in Dragnet reruns.

"Ronnie? What's going on?" Beverly asked. He looked as if he was about to cry.

"You believed in me when I no longer

believed in myself," Ronnie said. "Thank you." He sniffed his emotions back. "I gotta go to jail now. But I am so sorry I didn't recognize you earlier."

"What do you mean, Ron?" Beverly studied him, carefully. He certainly seemed sincere. Maybe, he actually was sincere.

"I once fell so low I asked God why I should go on living. He took so long to answer, I figured he forgot about me. So when he did answer, I missed it. I missed you. And I'm so sorry. I love you so much. I just hope you'll give me another chance."

Beverly looked deep into Ronnie's eyes. They were soulful and filled with honesty. The kind of eyes a husband should have. The kind of eyes a man who would set up a trust fund for his mother should have. The kind of eyes a man who let his brother pretend to own a home would have. Beverly's defenses melted away.

"It's my policy," Beverly began. "All my husbands get two chances." She opened her arms, and embraced him.

Misty growled.

Ronnie put the cat to the ground and returned Beverly's embrace.

Misty shot off back into the house, followed by a very enthusiastic pack of dogs.

Captain Jones leaned against his patrol car and glanced over at Oprah. "You still want to press charges?

"Of course!" Oprah returned.

Captain Jones was about to make his way toward the perp when Cliff tugged at his sleeve. "Sir, captain? Pleeeease?"

"Knock yourself out," Jones said, permitting

his partner his very first ever arrest. Cliff practically skipped up the stairs, handcuffs at the ready, Miranda Rights firing off in his head. He hoped he would remember them.

Ronnie took Beverly's face in his hands. "I'll explain all of this later. Don't worry about me, okay? Go on inside. Enjoy the party."

Beverly cast a glance inside the house or, to put a finer point on it, the total apocalypse inside the house. Not to be harsh, but what party was Ronnie thinking of? Poor guy.

"You have the right to remain silent," Cliff sang as he slapped the cuffs on Ronnie. "Anything you say can and will be held against you in a court of law!" Cliff ran through the remaining items with the expertise of a veteran stage actor.

As Ronnie was led to the patrol car, he called back to the house. "Freda, sorry about the mess!" Ronnie caught Oprah's eye as Cliff opened the rear door. "Oprah, sorry about the dogs, and by the way, I get it now." Ronnie turned for a moment to the officers of the fine states of Indiana and Illinois. "Sorry, I didn't stop. Merry Christmas, everyone!"

Cliff put his hand on Ronnie's head, as was regulation when stuffing a suspect into the back seat, when the suspect resisted. Ronnie had one more apology to offer to Oprah's bodyguard. Bud had mysteriously been missing in action the entire time, but now, here he was, and after this, Ronnie's To Do list would be complete.

"Sorry about kicking you in the nuts!"

Cliff replaced his hand on his prisoner's head.

Oprah turned to Bud. Not only did she want to know where the hell he had been, she wanted to know why the kidnapper knew him.

"Well?" she asked.

"I was at sensitivity training. I didn't want anyone to know."

"And?"

Bud leaned over to Oprah and whispered in her ear.

"Are you serious?" she asked.

Bud nodded. Ashamed.

"Hey!" Oprah yelled, just as Officer Cliff was stuffing Ronnie into the car. They paused. Oprah strode up to them and looked at Ronnie. "Anyone ever tell you you've got a great jawline?"

Ronnie took a moment to think about it. No one had, as far as he knew.

* * *

Oprah's face filled the screen, her eyes soft and happy. The jazzy fusion with funky snare – now combined with a little bit of jingling bells – faded away as did the audience applause.

"For a couple days now, we've been looking for this woman," said Oprah. Her image was replaced with a photograph from the Chicago Hilton, wherein an unconscious Ronnie laid sprawled on the hallway next to the planter. "Well, we've found her." Oprah smiled big for the camera. "And, wait till you hear her Christmas story. Next, on Oprah."

The couple writhing underneath the bed sheets weren't exactly tuned in to the Oprah Winfrey Show broadcast. Yet, it made for good background noise.

"Yeow!" Butter's voice came from beneath the covers. "Turn it down!"

Shenique's voice was muffled as she replied, "What's a matter? Can't take it?"

The *zap* from her Panther Stun Gun was muffled, too. Just not as much.

"Here, you try it," offered Butter.

Another *zap*.

"Yaah! Okay, turn it down." Shenique agreed. Her hand slid out from the sheet, put the stun gun on the nightstand, and grabbed the remote control, instead.

It was hot and humid in what appeared to be a tropical paradise. A ceiling fan rotated lazily above a breakfast table filled with Ackee and saltfish, plantain, breadfruit, and boiled green bananas. Songs of doves and warblers filled the air.

Henry raised a glass of frothy soursop juice to Denise and clinked his rim to hers.

"Whisked away to a tropical paradise with my handsome Jamaican Prince." Denise sipped, then put her glass down. "I'm so happy you called me back."

"Ya know, I'm glad I did, too."

They drank again.

Outside their window, a flurry of snow blew across the pane.

A banner flapped against the framework of a corner store on Hyde Park Street. It announced to all passers-by that the Beverly Mitchell Photography & Gallery was coming soon. There was just one picture for display at this time; others would soon follow, but this one was special. It was the extraordinary image of Grant Park that Beverly had taken from her hotel room. At the bottom of the picture, in gold ink, was the signature, "*Beverly Mitchell*".

Next to the soon-to-be-opened gallery: *Mitchell Investments*. The sign was stenciled in the same golden pen.

Ronnie and Beverly stood arm in arm, looking on at the new chapters about to be opened in their lives. They were accompanied by the little girl from the Way of the Light Mission, the one who had complimented Ronnie on his pants suit, and the girl's mother, Bonita. Bonita dabbed a kerchief at her eyes.

"You start right after the New Year," Ronnie said. "Fifteen dollars an hour, healthcare, and a 401K."

Bonita nodded and sniffled. "Thank you, Mister Mitchell."

The little girl tugged at Ronnie's hand. "Thanks for giving my mommy a job."

"I'm just glad I can, sweetie. Do you like your new apartment?"

The girl nodded, her little pigtails bouncing on her head in joyful cadence. "I've never had my own room!"

A raspy voice came from above. "Good, you're still here," Gretta's gravely tone lofted down from one of the second story apartments. "I was wondering…. Could I keep a pet?"

"Um, sure," Ronnie said. "Just nothing too loud."

Gretta ducked her head back inside.

Beverly leaned close to Ronnie and

whispered.

"Hey, Gretta?" Ronnie called. Gretta poked her head back out. "What are you doing for dinner?"

The home of Linda and Jeff Mitchell was the destination for this year's holiday supper. Normally Freda and Ted would have hosted such an event, but theirs was in the half-way stages of repair and reconstruction. Their last festivities took a toll on their interior design.

A Christmas tree stood like a sentry in the living room, surrounded by mountains of brightly wrapped presents. A gentle fire roared in the hearth that was topped with rows and rows of over-filled stockings. The flat screen above the fireplace was broadcasting the last of The Oprah Winfrey Holiday Special.

Freda passed around a tray of roasted chestnuts, purchased from the specialty shop downtown. Ted and Jeff helped themselves to a handful, as Linda double-checked on the dairy-free egg nog in the punch bowl. Mrs. Mitchell sat in her new rocking chair and thought how nice it would have been to have a grandbaby napping on her substantial lap. Elliott and Wanda Bunn, sitting beside Mrs. Mitchell and sharing a chocolate Santa with marshmallows, harbored the same sentiment. Ah, well. There's always next year.

Ronnie stood up and tapped his spoon against his hot cocoa mug. Beverly gave him a reassuring nod of support. He looked a little nervous, as well he should be.

"Everyone?" Ronnie asked and tugged at his

necktie. "I have something for all of you."

A hush fell on the living room. Ronnie felt as though he was in a particularly hot, particularly uncomfortable spot light.

"Hey, Ron. Just having you out of jail and here with us is the best gift we could have," Ted said as he cracked open a walnut.

"Thanks," said Ronnie and proceeded to pull out a stack of envelopes from his dress jacket. I've been a little bogus this past year, and I want to thank you guys for being there for me."

Ronnie made his way through his family, handing out the envelopes, all hand written in golden pen. Freda tore hers open, and pulled out a stack of cash.

"Freda, Ted, that's for taking care of Butter."

Freda shook her head. "Ronnie, you didn't have to do this."

"Jeff, Linda..." Ronnie began as they looked up at him. "That's the money I borrowed, with interest. Calculated at ten-point-five percent APR, with proration up to, and including, today."

"Ronnie.... wow," Linda remarked, running the calculation in her head to ensure it was correct before looking up for help from Jeff. "I don't know what to say."

Mrs. Mitchell stopped rocking as Ronnie approached her. "Mom? This is to repay you for the cost of hiring those Man-Away guys. And to thank you. I needed that."

"Damn right you did," Mrs. Mitchell returned.

Beverly beamed at Ronnie. Here he was, acting grown up and humble, and all the things she knew he could be. The Best He Could Be.

Unexpectedly, however, he was now standing in front of her, a look on his face that she couldn't describe. They had rehearsed his speech for a couple of days before now, even blocking out the order in which his envelopes would be distributed. But this was something they hadn't gone over. Ronnie handed her a special envelope, embossed in silver and gold.

"And that's every dime I took out of your accounts and ran up on your credit cards," he said, and then got down on one knee. He took a small velvet box from his pocket and opened it. A beautiful ring shone, reflecting the lights from the tree and the fireplace. "This one's real."

Beverly put the ring on her finger. "Funny enough, it really doesn't matter. In fact," she said, admiring the larger cubic zirconia on her finger, "I'll keep this one. I'm not a real diamonds kind of girl." She took Ronnie's hands, and as he stood up beside her to move in for a kiss, she stopped him. "And since we're taking the time for unexpected announcements, I have one, too." Beverly held Ronnie's hand, tightly. "Speaking of expecting…" she put Ronnie's hand on her stomach. "We're pregnant."

Mrs. Mitchell's hands flew to her face. Wanda stared, mouth agape, as her husband grinned a toothy grin.

Ronnie and Beverly shared a passionate kiss, both of Ronnie's hands upon his wife's belly.

Above the fireplace, the audience attending the Oprah Winfrey Holiday Special cheered in wild yuletide appreciation. Oprah turned to her guest and waited for his closing thoughts.

"The lesson, for me," Ronnie began telling

Oprah, "was just to understand one really powerful truth. That it's alright to fail. It comes with learning to live. And it often leads to a better, more exciting path, if you just trust."

Oprah nodded. "And you know you're trusting when..."

"After you fail, you try again."

"Now you get it. That's great. Merry Christmas, everyone," Oprah said to her audience, both in the studio and at home.

The jazzy fusion and funky beat with the right amount of jingle began as the camera scanned the audience. Underneath every seat, golden envelopes from Oprah herself were discovered. God bless them. Every one.

Beverly, Mrs. Mitchell, and Wanda put the last of the dishes in the washer. Mrs. Mitchell and Wanda were delighted beyond measure to express concerns for Beverly's bending and stooping, but she assured them she was happy to do it. For come next Christmas, she'd have her hands full. Ronnie came in, the last of the egg nog glasses on a tray, when the doorbell rang.

"I'll get it," he said, gave Beverly a quick kiss, and placed the tray upon the counter.

Dana waited on the front stoop and wiped the fog from her glasses.

Ronnie opened the door. The smile that was etched on his lips all day disappeared.

"Hi, Ronnie," Dana said at last. "Ronnie... I was in New York this morning and caught you on

Oprah. I realized how much I hurt you. I can't be the best me with that on my conscious. So I'm here to ask your forgiveness."

"You're joking, right?" Ronnie asked. He even went so far as to look around for the cameras he believed to be there. Like he was being punked for Christmas.

"I wouldn't have flown eight hundred miles for a joke, Ronnie."

Ronnie nodded. Dana was a serious woman. Always had been, always would be. "Okay," he said. "Sure. You're forgiven. Have a good life, Dana."

"Thank you, Ronnie," Dana sighed. "You, too."

Dana turned back to the street, to the limo that was waiting at the curb. It was a hell of a long way to travel for a ten second exchange of dialogue, but to her, it was worth it. Now she could get on with being her Best. Closure was a great gift to give herself.

"Dana!" Ronnie shouted from the porch.

She turned around. *SMASH!* A snowball exploded in her face, the powder wedged between her right eyeglass lens and her right eye. Her left eye and lens was clear. She glared at Ronnie with her good eye.

"Merry Christmas!" Ronnie yelled as he crafted another snowball.

Dana turned to run toward her waiting limo. She ripped open the door just as the second snowball slammed into the back of her head!

"And Happy New Year!"

The End

If you enjoyed this book, please take a moment to write your review on Amazon and your favorite book site. Thank you—TRL.

CPSIA information can be obtained
at www.ICGtesting.com
Printed in the USA
BVHW030202061118
532303BV00001B/60/P